But sex is a difficult passion to handle," he said to Sarah. "Sensuality an insidious weapon. I thought that in that field you weren't too well prepared. That its earthier aspects were outside your experience."

"All right, you win," Sarah said quietly. For how could she tell him that she ached to feel his arms around her, that frustration and unhappiness at the situation between him and Anna, with all its uncertainties and contradictions, caused her heart to ache as painfully as his at this moment.

And Anna's insinuation that he kept her around for convenience, false though she felt it was, still galled her as though it were a blatant denial of her identity.

The Aston Hall Romance Series:

- #101 *Night of a Thousand Stars*
- #102 *Escape to Ecstasy*
- #103 *A Time in September*
- #104 *To Love a Stranger*
- #105 *Starfire*
- #106 *Doctors in Love*
- #107 *Shetland Summer*
- #108 *No Stars So Bright*
- #109 *The Scent of Rosemary*
- #110 *A Distant Song*
- #111 *Roses Out of Reach*
- #112 *Summer at Hope House*
- #113 *To Him Who Waits*
- #114 *One Love Lost*
- #115 *Someone to Love*
- #116 *Loving Partnership*
- #117 *Rough Weather*
- #118 *This Girl Is Mine*
- #119 *Dancing in the Shadows*
- #120 *Gentle Lover*

WRITE FOR OUR FREE CATALOG

If there is a Pinnacle Book you want—and you cannot find it locally—it is available from us simply by sending the title and price plus 75¢ to cover mailing and handling costs to:

Pinnacle Books, Inc.
Reader Service Department
271 Madison Avenue
New York, NY 10016

Please allow 6 weeks for delivery.

_____Check here if you want to receive our catalog regularly.

Iris Bromige
A DISTANT SONG

PINNACLE BOOKS   LOS ANGELES

This is a work of fiction. All the characters and events portrayed in this book are fictional, and any resemblance to real people or incidents is purely coincidental.

A DISTANT SONG

Copyright © 1977 by Iris Bromige

All rights reserved, including the right to reproduce this book or portions thereof in any form.

An original Pinnacle Books edition, published by special arrangement with Aston Hall Publications, Inc.

First printing, October 1980

ISBN: 0-523-41117-0

Printed in the United States of America

PINNACLE BOOKS, INC.
2029 Century Park East
Los Angeles, California 90067

CHAPTER ONE

THE GRASS IN the park, a rich green again now, refreshed by the autumn dews after the long, hot summer, was already sprinkled with the first leaves of autumn. In the flower beds, dahlias glowed richly in the October sunshine. The brown-haired girl sitting on a seat near the intersection of two paths reflected that these symbolized aptly the present stage in her life. She was at a crossroads, undecided which way to take. The subdued noise of traffic reached her from the perimeter of the park. At her feet, a group of hopeful sparrows hopped and pecked and squabbled and then flew off at the approach of a yapping terrier straining on a lead. Peace restored, she turned her mind to making a detached review of her present situation in the hope that it would help her to arrive more easily at a decision.

Here she was, at twenty-five, Sarah Rushden, editorial assistant in a firm of publishers, author of one book for children published six months ago with very modest results, living in a minuscule flat in London. She knew that she was competent at her job, she enjoyed pleasant relations with her working associates, but of late she had become increasingly aware of the unreality of it all, as though she were playing a part and the real Sarah Rushden was lost under the scenery and costumes, that buried away was a quite different person: shy, hungry for a life of different quality that would not make her feel like a stranger acting a part in a play she did not care for. Now, an odd turn of events offered her a new road which she hesitated to take, and the main reason for her hesitation was the man she was meeting for lunch that day and whose advice she sought.

She had first met Nicholas Barbury two years ago at a cocktail party given by his literary agent soon after the successful launching of his first biography. She had been standing in for her then employer, who avoided such functions with great guile and determination. A tenuous friendship had developed, and emboldened by this, she had shown him the manuscript of the book she had written for children.

Nick, who had started out as a journalist and had won some renown as the editor of an arts magazine, was now, with the success of his second book confirming his high quality as a biographer, well established on the literary scene, and she had hesitated to burden him with her small effort. But he had been both encouraging and helpful, pointing out weaknesses with a gentle touch and giving a personal recommendation for the revised work to his literary agent, who had placed the book with a publisher.

And over those two years, her affection for Nick had grown deeper, and if he had ever given her any sign that his own feelings toward her were more than that of a kindly mentor, she knew that there would be no decision to make about a new road—for she would stay where she was, in touch with him.

She sighed and glanced at her watch. Time to be moving if she was to be punctual. She would make up her mind, she thought, after this meeting with Nick.

She was only a minute late, but he was there before her, chatting to the receptionist in the foyer of the hotel he had chosen for lunch. Her heart gave its usual little leap of pleasure when she saw him. Fair, with classically handsome features, always elegantly dressed, with a faintly husky, drawling voice, Nicholas Barbury might give an impression of effeteness to a stranger, but a few minutes in his company revealed a shrewd intelligence. He was as exasperating as he was charming, for his cool detachment never wavered, and what lay under the elegant surface remained hidden from her. She wondered if anybody had penetrated it. It seemed somehow typical of her way of life that she should be half in love with a man who was still essentially unknown to her, as though she lacked the capacity or opportunity to come to grips with anything or anybody.

"Well, Sarah," he said with a smile, "you look very refreshing in spite of these weighty problems you want to discuss with me."

"Good of you to answer my appeal so promptly."

"I've booked a table for half an hour from now. Thought we'd have a drink in the lounge while you unburden yourself. A pity to spoil a good lunch with weighty matters. Bad for the digestion."

Upstairs in the lounge they found a table in a quiet corner and Nick ordered two sherries. Then, leaning back in his armchair, he said, "Now, let's have it, my dear. What's the problem?"

"My grandfather died recently. He left me a cottage in Sussex. I went down to see it last weekend. I'm tempted to throw up my job and go down there and write."

Nick's eyebrows went up.

"And live on what?"

"Grandfather also left me a small legacy. I could live on it for a year, perhaps."

"Sounds romantic but might well prove the reverse. What sort of place is it? Isolated?"

"A downland hamlet. One shop, an inn, and a church. About two miles from a sizable village. Amazingly little changed from the days when I knew it as a child. I used to spend all my vacations there with my grandparents. I was only nine years old when I spent my last holiday there and hadn't seen it since, so I expected changes from the cottage of my memories. But except that it looked smaller than I remembered and very neglected, nothing else seemed to have changed much."

"That must be a record, then. Dangerous to go back to places. They've always changed for the worst with progress, it seems."

"Well, of course, it wasn't the happy, living place I remembered. I loved my holidays there. They were the happiest times I've ever known. My grandparents were dears, and Grandfather was friendly with the owner of a rambling old manor house on the outskirts of the hamlet. His name was Paul Rannock."

"I seem to know it. Wait a minute. Didn't he write a book on tribal cultures, or am I thinking of somebody else?"

"Could be. He was a great explorer in his time, I believe, but I only have a vague recollection of him. He had four children, though, and we became friends, so that I had company when I was on holiday. Mr. and Mrs. Rannock remain dim, but the Rannock children remain vivid in my memory. Perhaps because I was an only child and often lonely, so their companionship was especially memorable."

"Are they still there?"

"I don't know. I'm talking about sixteen or more years ago. We wouldn't know each other if we met now. My grandmother died when I was ten, and Grandfather left the cottage in the care of a housekeeper, went abroad, and never came back there to live. I believe my parents had an occasional letter from him, but as far as I was concerned, he faded from my life. I was sorry. I loved him. But it's a long time ago."

"You could keep the place for a holiday home. Rent it out, perhaps, when you don't want it."

"I think I'd like to try living there, and writing."

"You're not satisfied with your life now?"

She hesitated, trying to put the intangible dissatisfactions into words.

"I'm not really involved in it. Not me. The real me. I don't really belong. I'm all right as long as I keep busy. When I stop, I feel it's all unreal. Alien."

" 'I, a stranger and afraid
  In a world I never made.' "

"Who wrote that?"

"Housman. I thought you liked your job."

"It's very different since the takeover. Being one of a large group has changed our small family firm into an impersonal commercial enterprise. And the policy has changed. The emphasis now is on educational books, travel guides, art and technical books. Almost anything except fiction."

"And for you, a romantic, that has taken away the bloom," said Nick with a little smile.

"Nothing creative. All factual. That's not what literature is about."

"Agreed. But winter in an isolated cottage could be bleak. Are you resourceful? You'd need to be."

"I could be, I think. I'm not just an idealistic dreamer, you know, seeing roses round the cottage door. Is that how you see me?"

"I'm not being uncomplimentary when I say you look the part," said Nick, his eyes teasing her. "Stars in your eyes. But I've learned never to sit in judgment. We can all find inner resources in ourselves that we never knew we possessed until we were challenged, so how can an outsider judge?"

Sarah, inwardly wincing at the word outsider, and a little nettled by his indulgent attitude, eyed him with the exasperated ache which was becoming all too familiar when she was with him nowadays, and said firmly, "I'm not just seeking an escapist's retreat. When I went over the cottage last weekend, I came across an old trunk full of exercise books and papers and discovered that Grandfather had kept a journal for most of his life. Besides that, there were letters, newspaper clippings, magazines, a whole record of the life of his times. I wasn't there long enough to go into it in detail, but I wonder if at one time he meant to write his autobiography. He used to write plays for us to act, and I believe he wrote poetry, too. He always sent us birthday and Christmas cards with appropriate verses in them which he'd composed. That is, until Grandma died, when he seemed to dry up."

"Now that's very interesting," said Nick, his eyes alert now. "And explains where you get your writing itch from, no doubt."

"It occurred to me that in that trunk I could find all the material I needed to write children's books set back at the beginning of this century. The Edwardian period is one that has always attracted me. Perhaps because I feel a bit of a misfit in the modern scene," she concluded ruefully.

"I think you've got something there. There's a mood of nostalgia today, and kids like what they term 'old-fashioned' books, according to a cousin of mine who runs a library."

"Do you think I could do it, Nick? My first book hasn't done very well."

"You have to learn the job, and with writing, you can only learn by keeping on. I think you could do it admirably because your heart would be in it. All objections canceled. Go down to your cottage and get to work. You'll find a way of keeping yourself fed and warm, no doubt, and it's every writer's dream to be left alone undisturbed to get on with his work."

"True. When you come back from your imaginary world, though, it can sometimes feel chilly and lonely."

"You can't have everything."

"I'd like to feel I belonged in the real world, too. Had a stake in it. Have you ever thought of marriage, Nick?"

"I'm not a domestic type, my dear. I like my freedom."

"It's not a question of type, surely, but of loving."

"Some people are more self-sufficient than others. I'm a loner and like it that way. For you, Sarah, it will be different, I think. But don't underrate the importance of work you can be involved in. It's apt to wear better than people."

"That's a very sceptical remark."

"I need to keep those idealistic wings of yours from taking you up like a soaring lark. The drop from that height could be very painful."

But she was not inclined to let him elude her with generalities. At the crossroads, she wanted to know.

"I'm not talking about me. Have you never been in love? Wanted someone to share your life? You're always so cool, so detached, but I can't think you're as invulnerable as you appear."

"You're in a very probing mood today, Sarah."

"Telling me to mind my own business? But we're friends, Nick. When you're fond of people, you want to know more about them than what's on the surface. It's only natural."

"Very risky," he said lightly.

"I don't think so, with you. Underneath that charming cloak of yours, there is someone very worthwhile. I know that. I wish you'd take the cloak off sometimes."

"And you will promise me a beauteous day if I will travel forth without my cloak."

"Oh, Nick, must you always find a quotation to answer with," said Sarah, exasperated again.

"A terrible habit, I agree. One I'm always trying to curb. What do you want me to confess, Sarah? A long line of passionate, unfulfilled love affairs? I'm not a good subject for romance, my dear," he added gently.

So she had her answer. Her eyes met his, and she nodded, accepting it.

"A pity," she said lightly, changing the mood to avoid any awkwardness, although it would be rare, indeed, for Nicholas Barbury to be embarrassed. "I'd like to have heard about a love-strewn path if only to prove that you are humanly frail like the rest of us."

"Now that's a back-hander, if you like," he said, laughing. "Heart-to-hearts are not in my line, though. Prefer to keep my indiscretions to myself. But I should hate to spoil your day with nothing but dusty answers, so I'll try to soften your belief that I'm completely inhuman by saying that I *was* tempted to throw away my freedom once."

She looked up quickly.

"Why didn't you?"

"Because the lady in question was already committed to another, whom she subsequently married, fortunately for her because I should have made a terrible husband, and fortunately for me because I should have hated hurting her. She is very happily married, and I can enjoy vague sentimental memories without having had my chosen way of life destroyed. A satisfactory outcome for all parties."

"Do you see her still?"

"Occasionally. We're all good friends."

"How long ago was this?"

"Three or four years. It happened on vacation in Ireland, which explains my lapse. Ireland is a very romantic country, full of tragic history, ancient grudges, poetic myths, and a magic charm. Coupled with the intoxication of a beautiful landscape, there's something in the air that undermines common sense and reason and makes one liable to commit all sorts of follies. I consider I had a lucky escape."

"You're incorrigible. And lucky, too, perhaps, to know so clearly what you want of life."

"Well, I suppose in the end we get back as much or as little as we put into it. Now let's have some food. Enjoy a civilized meal while you can. The simple life awaits you."

Over lunch, he steered the conversation to impersonal topics. He was an amusing talker, and his cool, ironic picture of the literary scene soon had her laughing, her problems for the time being dismissed. It was not until the waiter poured their coffee that Nick returned to her personal affairs with his usual astuteness.

"Well, Sarah, the decision's made, is it?"

"Yes. I shall go."

"Good. It's the right one, I'm sure. You've nothing to lose and possibly a lot to gain. Experience, anyway. And I'm not one for accepting a pattern of life that doesn't satisfy. Break the pattern and try another. That's why I value freedom of action so highly. You can't break the pattern easily if other people are involved. Remember that, Sarah."

She nodded, smiling. But his blood ran cool, she thought. For so much of her life, she had been conscious of a loneliness of spirit, a longing for loving relationships. Her home had not provided them, and her job had brought her friendly acquaintances but nothing that penetrated the surface of her life. Only those holidays in Sussex with her grandparents had brought her a warmth of companionship, a loving climate, the recollection of which could still glow faintly across the years like the embers of a fire that had warmed a chilly traveler.

He walked back across the park with her on his

way to his flat in Kensington. They parted at the gates.

"Good luck, my dear. I'll look forward to seeing the first book of your Edwardian series in print."

His words seemed dismissive. The problem aired, a decision reached, he was withdrawing. As she watched him cross the road, slight, fair-haired, moving with lithe grace, and disappear round a corner, she knew that that road was closed to her. Ignoring the blank unhappiness that sat like a leaden lump inside her, she walked to her bus stop, resolutely turning her mind to rehearsing her interview with Mr. Milchester on Monday morning, when she would give her month's notice. He would not, she thought, be at all pleased. The Managing Director was not renowned for seeing anyone else's point of view. And hers proved no exception.

When she knocked at the door of his office and went in on that Monday morning, he gave her a chilly smile and waved her to a chair.

"Just one moment, Miss Rushden."

He was reading a document, frowning, and tapping a finger on his desk as he read. Sarah sat down and waited. He had fixed the time to see her, but it was characteristic that he should keep her waiting. She sometimes thought it was a ploy to unnerve people, for Mr. Milchester was a clever tactician. She regarded him with steady brown eyes. Since their small, friendly firm of publishers had been taken over, the new Managing Director had made many changes. A tall, thin man with aquiline features and gray hair, he brought to the business an accountant's mind rather than a publisher's, and although she respected him, she had never liked him. He was frowning, and she wondered what it was that displeased him in the contract he was reading. The terms too generous, perhaps.

He looked up, put the contract on one side, leaned

back in his chair, and said, "Now, what's the trouble?"

"No trouble, Mr. Milchester. I just wanted to give you my month's notice of leaving."

He raised his eyebrows and looked very discouraging.

"But that *is* trouble, Miss Rushden. Trouble for us. As a valuable member of our editorial department, we can ill spare you. Is it a question of salary?"

"Oh, no. I've recently inherited a cottage in Sussex and I've decided to live there and do some writing."

His eyebrows went up still farther, and he eyed her like a hard-pressed but patient headmaster.

"Now come, Miss Rushden. I'm sure you're not as impractical as you sound. You have, I believe, had one book for children published. Corrie & Birch took it, didn't they?"

"Yes."

"Very creditable. But you know enough about the business, and have doubtless had your knowledge confirmed by your own experience now, to realize that your earnings from writing are going to be very modest indeed unless and until you achieve a bestseller. I don't believe, but you must correct me if I am wrong, that your first book has achieved those dizzy heights."

Sarcasm, thought Sarah darkly, will get you nowhere, Mr. Milchester. Her voice was honeyed as she replied, "Far from it. But I want to give all my time to writing for as long as my means allow, and I also want to get out of London. I've worked here for five years now. I feel I need a change."

"So restless, you young people. Once you're trained and of real value, you throw up your job and go elsewhere. I must say that this proposed move of yours sounds more than usually ill-advised and reckless, though. Have you really thought it through? Your prospects here are quite good, you know."

"I have thought it through, and my mind is made

up, Mr. Milchester. I'll do all I can to help anybody you may appoint in my place, of course."

"Very well. If I can't dissuade you from this foolish venture, there's no more to be said. There are one or two people on the staff who would not have surprised me with such a hare-brained venture, but I thought you were a sensible young woman. However . . ." He lifted his hands and shrugged resignedly, then said coldly, "Perhaps you'll ask Miss Lancing to come in."

He turned back to the contract and Sarah left him. Standing at the window of her office a few minutes later, she stared down at the maelstrom of traffic, at the high concrete wall of offices opposite, at the people on the pavements, dwarfed by the buildings, hurrying about their business like preoccupied ants, and felt a stir of excitement at the thought of the cottage in Sussex, the store of papers which would throw light on a past age, and the recollection of the happiness she had known there in her childhood.

It was time for a change. The challenge fired a new energy in her, bringing her to life after too long a period of acquiescence in a way of existence that was not unpleasant but merely meaningless to the Sarah Rushden who lived behind the public face. Her discussion with Nick and the attitude of Mr. Milchester had reinforced the choice which had been half made the previous weekend when she had first seen the cottage, shabby, overgrown, but the surroundings miraculously unchanged. She had been overwhelmed by memories of the past, so that she had seen through a mist of tears the ghosts of five children playing there, felt again for a fleeting moment the warmth and security of her grandmother's care, the enchantment of explorations of the countryside under the gentle guidance of her grandfather. And at nine years old it had all been cut off, the door locked.

A pneumatic drill had started up in the road

below, its bruising noise recalling her to the present. The wind in the trees of the cottage garden would make a welcome change. She turned back to her desk, happy and excited at the prospect before her, eager, now, to be gone.

CHAPTER TWO

AS THE SOUND of the hired car that had driven her the ten miles from the station faded away, Sarah picked up her case and went through the white wicket gate of Rylands and up the overgrown gravel path to the square brick and tile-hung cottage of her childhood memories. It was unpretentious but pleasing in the afternoon sunshine of that November day, its bricks mellow, its tiles mossy, its porch overhung with a tangled rambler rose, which still sported one or two straggling white blooms. The small leaded panes of the windows gave the cottage a cozy but guarded look, keeping the outside world at a distance.

Inside, she remembered, it had always been the smell of wax polish that had welcomed her, but now it smelled musty and dusty. The old housekeeper, who had been clinging to the cottage only out of a sense of duty to her absent employer, had relinquished it with relief and had departed the previous week to share a flat with her sister in Lewes. She had left it reasonably tidy, but the home was a travesty of what it once had been, and its restoration would be in a sense a tribute to her grandparents. She viewed the task before her with enthusiasm, tempered by the knowledge that although the spirit was eager, the money available was modest.

It was with this thought in mind that, over a pot of tea, she studied the letter that had arrived two days earlier.

Dear Sarah,

By an odd chance, Paul Rannock's name came up when I had lunch with my publisher yesterday. He is trying to persuade Rannock to write his memoirs. He's had a fantastic life of exploration, apparently, which would make a fascinating book. Rannock, not enthusiastic, says he might tackle it if he had the help of a ghostwriter and research assistant. Feels a bit beyond the effort himself.

Wondered whether you might like to keep the wolf from the door by offering your help. You're well qualified for the job, which would probably only be part-time. Anyway, it's up to you. Perhaps your own Edwardian saga is going to absorb all your time. Paul Rannock still lives in the same house, though, so it would be handy.

If you think anything of it, James Lexington will be happy to recommend you to Rannock on the strength of my glowing description of your editorial capabilities, or you might prefer the direct approach.

Over to you.

Yours,
Nick

Paul Rannock. Try as she would to delve back into the past, she could barely recollect him. A big man, she vaguely remembered, with a deep voice. On the few occasions when he had come to the cottage, he had remained closeted with her grandfather, a strange, remote being as far as she was concerned. But the children—Simon, Alison, Brian, Katie—she could see now, playing in the garden, toiling up the downs on blackberry expeditions, fishing on the river bank, jabbering noisily around the big wooden table in the kitchen while they demolished the splendid teas her grandmother had produced for them.

Simon, the eldest, six years older than she, was dark-eyed, black-haired, quick-tempered, and apt to be bossy; Alison, pale-faced, with long straight fair hair and a quiet, matter-of-fact air; Brian, who was the same age as Sarah, fair-haired with a quirky face and a lively, teasing temperament; and Katie, the youngest, whom Sarah had loved and who had a strange, wild beauty that set her apart. With her thick black tousled hair and large dark gray eyes in a face that was always chalkwhite even on the hottest summer day, her socks always hanging over her sandals, her clothes usually in need of repair, she combined a tomboy temperament with a wild grace and vivid imagination that Sarah had found irresistible.

She wondered what had happened to them. Whether they would recognize each other if they met. She would recognize Kate, she was sure. That light in her eyes, that magic something that set her apart. But she had seen them all through the eyes of a child. A lonely child, grasping eagerly at the easy friendship they offered. She had never gone to the Rannock home. They had always come to the cottage, drawn perhaps by the warmth and kindliness of her grandparents from a home run by housekeepers for an invalid mother and a father who spent most of his time abroad.

After a week spent in cleaning up the cottage and arranging the few personal belongings, mostly books, which she had brought with her, she was better able to assess what needed to be done there after so many years of neglect, and it was partly a vague desire to build a bridge between her childhood and her return to the same scene and partly the need to fortify her finances, which seemed all the more modest now that her commitments were clearer, that made her telephone Nick's publisher. He was delighted at her willingness to approach Paul Rannock.

"As you've had some connection with the family, I suggest you get in touch direct, and you can mention my name although your previous employer will guarantee your fitness for the job if Rannock wants more than my recommendation. He's an odd character. Doesn't seem all that keen on the project, so do your best to overcome his reluctance because I think it would make a splendid book."

"Is he at his home now?"

"Yes. He's given up traveling. Health not so good. Let me know how you get on. I got hold of a copy of your book after Nick told me about you. Promising. A sensitive touch. Keep at it."

Warmed by this little exchange, Sarah wrote to Paul Rannock the next day. It was a week before she had a reply.

> *My dear Sarah,*
> *So Martin's little granddaughter has come back to Rylands. And is now offering her services in the writing of my memoirs. What odd tricks life plays! Come along, my dear, and we'll talk about it. I suggest Saturday morning, at any time that suits you.*
> *Yours sincerely,*
> *Paul Rannock*

On the Friday evening before this appointment, Sarah was sitting before the fire with a plate of sandwiches on her lap and a pot of coffee on the hearth beside her. She had felt too tired to cook a meal after a strenuous day and now felt in a pleasantly relaxed mood as she watched the flames and wondered about her forthcoming interview with Paul Rannock. The room looked friendly and cozy and had responded well to her efforts. The old oak furniture now had a sheen on it, the faded cretonne curtains still retained some warmth of coloring after her washing had removed years of grime, the shabby green carpet had cleaned up reasonably well, and she had found a few late bronze chrysanthemums to bring life into the room. Fortunately, her grandparents had been of the generation that bought to last.

Accustomed to the silence and solitude of the past two weeks, she jumped at the sound of the doorknocker. She could not think who would be calling at eight o'clock that evening. Nobody so far had crossed the threshold of Rylands since her arrival, and she wondered if this might be the first visitor to break into her retreat.

It was a wild, blustery night, and she peered out into the darkness uncertainly. The porch light did not work, and the light from the little hall revealed only a tall man in a dark overcoat.

"Miss Rushden?" he said.

"Yes."

"Sarah Rushden. I'm Simon Rannock. Can I come in?"

"Simon! Of course."

He hung his coat up in the hall and followed her into the sitting room, standing just inside the door as he looked round him and said, "Just as I remember it. Lord, it's a long time ago!"

They stood looking at each other, trying to bridge the years. Only the deepset dark blue eyes beneath heavy black brows reminded Sarah of the boy. For the rest, this tall, lean man might have been a stranger. The spare bonework of the face was revealed now in place of the rounded contours of the boy; the thick black hair worn longer now than then; the beaky nose and firm mouth more sharply defined; the dark complexioned face more guarded than that of the volatile boy. There were lines around his eyes and mouth that made him look older than she knew he was, and she sensed a formidable hardness there that somehow shocked her and dissolved the cozy picture of the past. The most attractive thing about him, she thought, was the deep voice.

As though echoing her thoughts, he gave her an odd little smile and said, "The room's the same, but you don't call the child to mind."

"I was only nine when you last saw me."

"Shy, sensitive little Sarah Rushden, always looking as though she expected something wonderful round every bush."

"Those holidays always were wonderful to me."

"She looked so gentle that you were always surprised that she could on occasion prove so intractable."

"That was probably when you were using your extra years to be unacceptably bossy."

"Could be," he said, his eyes crinkling in the old way and momentarily softening the hardness of the new version of Simon Rannock.

"Will you have a cup of coffee? I've only just made it."

"Thanks. I'm sorry if I've interrupted your meal."

He refused any food and over coffee, in response to his inquiries, she told him why she had come to live in the cottage.

"So writing is your thing, is it? Not surprising, now I come to think of it. You always had a dreamy imagination, I remember. But this is rather a solitary life for a young woman, surely?"

"I'm used to living on my own. I had a flat in London."

"But that's a different kettle of fish altogether. You're pretty isolated here. Lonely for you."

"Loneliness is a state of mind. I felt lonely and a stranger in London all the years I was there."

"Your parents?"

"They died in a car crash when I was seventeen. I've been on my own ever since."

"I'm sorry."

"I missed my grandparents most of all. My mother and father . . ." She faltered, then went on, "theirs was not a happy marriage. Our home life was difficult. Somehow, this cottage was the only real home I knew. And it's warming to be back. My grandparents' affection seems to live on here. I feel at home, and I want to restore it to its old state as and when I can."

"Trying to recapture the past. Can't be done."

His firm dismissal irritated her, and her voice was cool as she said, "I'm here primarily to work on a book, undisturbed."

"Which brings me to the object of my call. This project of my father's. He's not really enthusiastic, and I think the effort would be a strain in his present poor state of health. He had a bad heart attack a year ago and has to take things very easily. To write his memoirs would entail a great deal of research into old diaries and maps of his explorations, and quite frankly I'd rather he wasn't encouraged to take it on."

"But he's not a child. He can surely make his own decisions."

"He wouldn't entertain it if he weren't bitten by some guilt complex about the way he neglected his family in the past. He thinks that if the book would make some money, as this publisher seems confident it would, he could leave us something when he dies. But none of us want him to undertake a task that will put a strain on him in order to have something to inherit."

"But he might enjoy writing about his past adventures and discoveries."

"He lived them. He's not interested in writing about them. He did write one book about remote native cultures just to put them on record, but he's not interested in revealing his life to the reading public. He never was an exhibitionist."

"He doesn't have to reveal his life. Only describe his explorations."

"They include painful episodes best forgotten. Anyway," he added impatiently, "he just doesn't want to do it. If the idea hadn't been put up to him by this publisher who happened to come across his one book, which has been out of print for years, it would never have entered his head. And if he wasn't suffering from this guilt complex and a feeling of making some recompense, he wouldn't entertain the idea now."

"Then where do I come in?"

"Don't offer your services. Without assistance, he won't, indeed can't, undertake it. And as he dislikes strangers and has become something of a recluse, he'll never seek an assistant."

"But I've already offered my services, and I'm seeing him tomorrow."

"I know. When he tells you what's involved, you can simply say that it's more than you feel able to tackle. Or not what you expected."

Sarah eyed him thoughtfully, not liking the manner in which he was disposing of other people's affairs.

"I don't think you have a right to interfere and make decisions for your father. He knows how you feel. It's up to him to decide."

"You don't understand what's involved. It will be subjecting him to a great strain."

"I could relieve him of that, perhaps, and a new interest in his life might prove beneficial."

"In other words, you think that you, a stranger, know better than I what is good for him."

"I distrust all people who know what is good for other people. It was a failing of yours when you were young, I remember. Your father is the best judge of his own affairs, I'm sure."

Simon Rannock was leaning back in his chair, surveying her with cool, appraising eyes. The verdict, she thought, was definitely unfavorable.

"Do you want the work? Financially, I mean."

"That wasn't the only reason I offered my services, but it was one of them."

"I see. It shouldn't be difficult to find part-time work in Dilford, you know. Not too far off."

"But not as near as Marlyn Manor, nor with a family connection which I remember with affection. My enthusiasm for commuting to a town has been exhausted, too," she said gently.

"I'm wasting my time in appealing to you, then?"

"I'm afraid so. The person to appeal to is your father. He decides, as far as I am concerned."

He subjected her to a silent scrutiny of some moments' duration. It unnerved her, and she busied herself with poking the fire to avoid his gaze. Then he said drily, "It's a pity to disturb old memories, destroy the old picture. Distance always seems to lend enchantment."

She tried to contain the spurt of anger, but tiredness from the day's exertions and this wounding disappointment at her first encounter with a member of the family she had idealized over the years weakened her control and sent discretion flying.

"Meaning exactly what?"

"Do you really want me to spell it out?" he asked calmly.

She might have remembered that he was the last person in the world to challenge. As a boy, he had always taken up any challenge and returned it with interest.

"Yes."

"I meant that memory has a way of blotting out the unpleasant and keeping alive and even exaggerating the pleasant aspects of the past. When you look back, the summers were always sunny and warm. You remember the laughter and fun of childhood friends, forget the rainy days, the boredom and quarrels and irritating characteristics of those same friends."

"You're bringing them to mind fast," she snapped.

She was not sure whether it was anger or amusement that brought a sparkle to his eyes.

"Well, it's a sad experience to go back to a place and find that time has shabbied and dimmed it, changed it for the worst, and to meet childhood friends and find that time has played the same trick with them."

"Do stop generalizing. I was nine years old and you were fifteen when we last met. You always were a bossy boy, but you were a good deal older than the rest of us, and it could be excused then. I see now that it's an entrenched characteristic."

"Too bad. As a matter of fact, I was growing out of you all at the end. At that point, the age gap was making itself felt. But I didn't come to reminisce over the past, only to ask you not to encourage my father to take on this work. Believe me, I have good reasons for asking this."

"I'll bear what you've said in mind when I talk to your father tomorrow. Then I shall use my own judgment."

"Very well," he said curtly, and stood up.

It had all gone wrong, she thought. She wanted to ask him about Alison, Brian, and Katie, but this grim stranger was unapproachable. Trying to make other people's decisions for them, not hiding the fact that he found the adult Sarah Rushden a disappointing version of the child, he seemed to her both arrogant and jaundiced. She accompanied him to the door in silence, and he gave her a brief "Goodnight" and disappeared into the darkness of the night.

Back in the sitting room, she tried to dismiss him from her thoughts by tuning in to a radio concert of Schubert's music, which she had been looking forward to, but, for once, the music did not hold her. Simon Rannock had broken into her peace and seclusion, had disturbed her warm image of the past, and lingered there like an unwelcome ghost. She was sorry that he had been the first visitor to Rylands.

CHAPTER THREE

THE BLUSTERY SOUTHWEST wind was still blowing the next morning when Sarah walked down the lane to keep her appointment with Paul Rannock. It whipped up the fallen leaves into sudden wild dances and brought the last shreds of foliage down from the tossing branches overhead. A fitful sun brushed the hedgerow, polishing the hawthorn berries, putting a fiery glow into the rose hips, turning the ivy leaves into mirrors of light. She breathed in the damp fragrance of the air, enjoyed feeling the wind lift her hair, and walked through the checkered pattern of sunshine and shadow wondering why she had allowed herself to be shut up in city streets for so many wasted years. Little by little, the old childhood enchantments of the country were unfolding themselves again, fragments of the knowledge about nature, which her grandfather had imparted to her with such love and enthusiasm, kept coming back to her, and always her eyes had beauty to feast on and her ears nothing strident to contend with.

Through a gateway in the hedgerow, she could see the river twisting on its quiet course, its surface rippled by the wind, reeds swaying along its banks. Once, she remembered, her grandfather had pointed out two otters swimming in that river after bass that had come in with the high tide.

She passed the one shop of the hamlet, which seemed to stock almost everything, then the church, the inn, and after a short climb came to the side road which led to Marlyn Manor, not nearly as grand as its name, but a rambling gray-stone building set in two acres of what were now overgrown grounds.

Her first impression of the house as the somewhat severe looking housekeeper led her across the large dark hall was a chilling one. She was ushered into a room at the back of the house and told that Mr. Rannock would be with her in a few minutes. The room was large, shabbily but comfortably furnished with a desk, armchairs, a table piled with papers, and bookshelves ranged around three sides of the room. She was looking out at the leaf-strewn lawn and enormous ash trees that dominated the garden when the same deep voice which she remembered from the past, and which his son had inherited, said, "Sarah Rushden. Forgive me for keeping you waiting, but I was caught on the telephone. Pernicious, intrusive instrument. Do sit down. So we've a Rushden back at Rylands after all these years."

She tried to hide the shock of his appearance. Tall, gaunt, broad-shouldered, his lined face was disfigured by a puckered scar running from eye-socket to jaw, and his mouth was drawn up on that side. His hair was white and in such a ravaged face the dark, deepset eyes burned with unexpected vitality. He limped and used a stick, which he laid aside as he lowered himself into the armchair opposite her.

"And Marlyn Manor still has the same owner," she said. "I was so glad when I learned that. The holidays I spent with my grandparents meant so much to me, and the Rannock children were part of it all."

"Your grandfather was my very dear friend. My only friend, really. You have his eyes. Rich brown, like a good glass of bitter."

"I wish he hadn't disappeared from my life when I was so young. I missed him, terribly."

"Everything changed for him when your grandmother died. He felt compelled to make an entirely different life. Became a roamer, like me. Amazing, really, because he was sixty-five when she died. Went on for another fifteen years, staying for short periods in all sorts of odd places, never able to settle. He was lucky in retaining his physical strength. He was fifteen years older than me, but he lasted a lot better."

"Your travels were more arduous, though."

"True. We lost touch eventually. I was sorry."

"After Grandma died, my parents heard from him hardly at all, and I never."

"He was very fond of you."

"As well as the cottage, I've inherited a trunk of papers and a journal he kept. There are entries up to the time Grandma died, but very sparse ones toward the end. The years of his youth, though, are very fully chronicled and fascinating."

Drawn out by his interest, she told him of her plans and only curbed her enthusiasm when she realized that they had met to discuss his memoires, not her plans. He waved her apologies aside with a twisted smile, which was oddly touching in its grotesqueness.

"Yours sounds a much more enjoyable proposition. I was born the year King Edward died, and I can still remember a little of World War I, so your grandfather's journal will cover ground familiar to me. If it wouldn't be intrusive, I'd like to see it some time."

Eventually, he brought up the question of his memoirs.

"Not a project I want to embark on, but I feel I owe it to the children to earn a little money to leave them if I can. Your help would be invaluable and give me the extra prod I need to tackle it."

"Are you sure your health is good enough to stand the effort?" she asked gently, and seeing his frown, added quickly, "I had heard that you were in poor health and had to lead a quiet life now."

"Who did you hear that from? Local gossip, I suppose. Why should I want to prolong a useless life by taking such care, sparing myself every effort? What sort of a life is that, for heaven's sake? Quality, not quantity, is what matters. This is a chance to do something that will be useful to my family, and if I'm not capable of sustaining any mental effort, it's time I was put down. Sorry. I didn't mean to be fierce."

"I understand how you feel. I should be of the same mind," she said, glad that he had not probed the source of her information since Simon's interference would obviously not have pleased him.

"I think we'd work well together, Sarah. Make a good team. What about it? Say three afternoons a week. Could you spare as much?"

Her eyes met his. There was a challenging life in them. He wasn't a cabbage. There was vitality there. It had a right to be used. It would seem insulting, diminish his stature by denying him that right. She smiled at him with a feeling of warm affection as she said, "I'd love to take it on."

"Splendid. Now, about terms. What do you suggest? You'll have realized by now that I'm hopelessly out of touch with such matters. Quite impractical where money's concerned, anyway."

"I think we could make it just a friendly arrangement. I can get by. Money between Rushdens and Rannocks doesn't seem right, somehow."

"Another hopelessly impractical person, I see. Won't do. You must never underrate your professional worth. That confounded publisher telephoned me again yesterday and made it clear that you were a first-class editor and could, if need be, write the book yourself. Such services command high pay these days, I'm sure."

"He wants to get the book from you," she said, smiling.

"Well, if you won't name a salary, we'll have to refer it to a third party. My son is more in touch with such matters. I'll consult him. You remember Simon, I expect. He disapproves of the whole project. It will please my perverted sense of humor to ask him to adjudicate."

"Does Simon live here with you or is he married?"

"He's not married. Works in Dilford. Has a flat there and comes here most weekends to keep an eye on things."

"What sort of work?"

"He's recently become a partner in a firm of architects. Helmsdale, Lymington and Rannock. A good team. He's out in the garden now, sawing up a tree that blew down last night. Like to go out and find him, my dear, and ask him to join us for coffee? I'll get Mrs. Pilsen to bring it in ten minutes' time. He'll be at the end of the garden behind the thicket."

The garden was carpeted with leaves, obscuring lawn, paths, and flower borders, the legacy of the numerous forest trees that grew along the boundaries. Many, many years ago, she thought, they were probably hedgerow trees marking the boundaries of fields. Now, the survival of the fittest had resulted in a near forest of oak, ash, and maple trees whose leaves she almost waded through toward the thicket of smaller trees at the end. In summer, she thought, the house must be darkened by the proximity of such enormous trees, and it needed little imagination to see the house swallowed up by them in the years to come. Now, the wind tossed the branches, played with the leaves, and sent fluffy clouds scudding across the sky like sheep on the run.

Simon, in shirt sleeves and slacks, was sawing up a small tree trunk with some difficulty.

"Hullo," said Sarah a little warily.

He looked up and straightened his back.

"Hullo. I shouldn't stand there if I were you. That

branch above you is only hanging by a strip of bark."

"I've been sent to ask you to come in for coffee," she replied, moving to safety.

"I'd sooner get this finished."

"Your father wants to consult you about the terms of my employment."

"You've accepted the job, then?"

"Yes."

"Then I don't think there's anything to consult me about."

"We can't agree about payment. I don't want to be paid for it. Your father insists. He doesn't know much about such matters and wants you to arbitrate. I hope you'll persuade him that money doesn't come into it."

"You weren't of that opinion last night."

"I know. But now that I've met your father, I feel money doesn't come into it. Not between your family and mine."

"Good grief! We only knew each other as kids on holiday, and you hardly ever saw my father. We hardly saw him, for that matter. Of course you must be paid for your services."

"There's no 'of course' about it. I can't explain how I feel, but you must just accept that I shall enjoy helping your father on three afternoons a week, and leave it at that."

"Such sentiments sound altruistic, but in reality they would put my father under an obligation to you and allow you to treat it as a kind of hobby with no prescribed duties."

"You seem to have a low opinion of people's motives."

"I like things clear-cut. Otherwise, nobody knows where they stand. On an unpaid basis, my father would hesitate to give any instructions, and you would feel free to back out any time it suited you. A woolly-minded arrangement. I'm not in favor of the project at all, as you know, but if you've encouraged my father to embark on it, for heaven's sake let's have a cut-and-dried arrangement to make it as easy for him as possible."

"You know, I find the implications of your attitude rather objectionable."

"Not meant to be," he replied calmly. "The laborer is worthy of his hire. And are you so well off that such a vulgar thing as money doesn't enter into your life? I gathered that you needed part-time work for financial reasons."

"Only because the cottage has been so neglected and I want to restore it. But that can wait until I see how my literary earnings turn out. I've enough to live on for a year. I like your father. I shall enjoy doing this for him. For friendship, if you like. For old times' sake."

His expression softened as he looked at her, shaking his head.

"I believe you mean it. What romantic foolishness! You haven't grown up much, have you? Still the old out-of-this-world Sarah, full of romantic illusions laced with the quiet tenacity of a mole."

"Is a mole tenacious?"

"Try and get one out of a lawn."

"Then you'll have to bear with me and let me have my way on this matter of payment. A basis of employer and employee just doesn't come into it as far as I'm concerned."

"I shan't back you on this, but unfortunately when I'm faced with two romantics, I'm not too sanguine about my chances. This saw's about as much use as a nail file. Not a decent tool to be found in this place," he said disgustedly, as he flung the offending article down on a wooden bench outside the toolshed.

"Is your father a romantic?"

"You don't need me to confirm that. You've sensed it already. That's the reason for this instant *rapport* between you. His whole life bears it out. A romantic through and through, and other people have paid for it, unfortunately. That bell sounds like Mrs. Pilsen at her least endearing. We'd better go."

He pulled on the sweater he had hung on the branch of a nearby tree and they walked back to the house, more at ease with each other than before. Perhaps the hard physical work had improved his temper, she thought. As though sensing this, he said abruptly, "I'm sorry if I was a bit gritty last night. There are things involved that you know nothing about. Unreasonable of me to expect you to agree with my attitude without that knowledge."

"Why didn't you share it with me, then?"

"Private and personal to my father. I'd forgotten how stubborn you could be, and I'm afraid I wasn't in a wheedling mood. Now that I'm reminded of your romantic attitude toward the Rannocks, though, I realize that the first encounter was a bit harsh."

"That's all right. I wouldn't have known you, anyway, if you'd come as a wheedler. That was never part of your makeup."

"Sawing up trees is a dirty job," he observed as they went into the hall. "I'll be with you in five minutes."

Over coffee, Simon reiterated his disapproval of the whole idea but yielded when his father said quietly, "You mustn't oppose my one chance of making amends for past neglect. Inadequate amends, I know, but something. It will give some purpose to my present useless life."

But the joint opposition of Simon and his father could not shake Sarah's decision that this should be a friendly arrangement, not a business transaction.

"Very well, my dear, if that is what you really wish," said Paul Rannock. "There will be other ways of repaying you, perhaps. I'm grateful for your offer. It's going to be a very agreeable collaboration, I'm sure. Now stop pouring cold water on the project, Simon, and pour me another cup of coffee instead."

"I know when I'm beaten," replied Simon with a shrug. "I wash my hands of two such impractical people. One thing I do ask, though, Dad. If it's a strain on you in any way, please don't continue. Don't put yourself under any stress as a sort of penance."

Their eyes met and Paul Rannock nodded slowly.

"Yes, you have the right to ask that, Simon. I'll be sensible. Now, Sarah, tell us more about this journal your grandfather kept. I think Martin was the wisest man I've ever known. Anything he wrote would be worth reading."

They chatted on about her grandfather for a little while, and then Sarah took her leave. Simon walked down the drive with her.

"You've made a hit with my father," he said abruptly. "He's become a recluse. Haven't seen him warm to any outsider for years. You've got through to him."

"Because of his friendship with my grandfather, perhaps."

"Could be. He's always been a loner, of course, but your grandfather meant a lot to him. Almost the only personal bond he formed in his whole life. Lord, what a shambles this place is," he added, kicking his way through a deep drift of leaves.

"It's a large place for one man to live in."

"Yes, but he couldn't bear to be fenced in now."

"Your brother and sisters, Simon. I've heard no mention of them."

"We're pretty scattered. Alison is married and has a child. A daughter of five. They live in Surrey. Brian was in the Isle of Wight last time we heard, but he's never in one place for long. Likes to change jobs frequently."

"What sort of jobs?"

"At the moment, I believe he's secretary to some golf club. He favors leisure industries."

Sarah was not encouraged by his dry tone to probe further into Brian's activities, but said eagerly, "And Katie? Dear Katie."

"An actress. In a provincial repertory company at present."

"That sounds right for the Katie I remember. Such a vivid personality. Young as she was when I knew her, she had star quality for me."

"We seem to have made an extraordinary impact on you, for you to remember us so well after all these years. Blessed if I can recall kids I knew at prep school in any but the vaguest terms. I think you've enshrined us in rosy veils all these years. I've removed one, I'm afraid, so perhaps you'd better keep the others intact and not inquire further. Sentimentalists need to keep their distance if they're not to be shaken by reality."

"What a Jonah you are!"

"Perhaps just indulging my protective instincts. For old times' sake," he added wickedly.

She smiled and shook her head at this little jab. She was happy at the morning's outcome and was not to be put down. He laid a detaining hand on her arm as she turned to go.

"Sarah, if when you're working with my father, you notice any signs of strain, will you let me know? I'm only here at weekends, not always then, and he'll conceal it from me if he can. I have good reasons for asking."

"Yes, of course I'll let you know. It's the last thing I'd want. But it might prove a tonic, you know."

"I think not."

"You haven't told me everything, have you?"

"Not quite. One day, perhaps. It should come from my father, if anybody."

"I'll keep a watchful eye."

"Thanks."

As she walked back down the lane, she found it difficult to equate the old Simon with the new. She caught a glimpse now and again of the boy in the man, but there was a hardness now which repelled her and made it difficult to assess what was underneath. One thing was certain. He had never seen *her* through any rosy veils, had scarcely remembered her, and now found her a foolish, sentimental and obdurate intruder. Dismissing this sour little apple of disappointment from her thoughts, she dwelled on the pleasanter discovery of Paul Rannock and the sympathy which had sprung up between them. She would enjoy working with him and hoped she could bring some interest into the life of this lonely, ravaged man.

Simon, rejoining his father, found him sorting the pile of papers on the table.

"There are two more boxes of papers in the attic, Simon. If you could fetch them down some time today, I'll try to get them into some sort of order. A delightful young woman, that. Her grandfather's genes are dominant in her, that's certain. A stroke of luck, her coming out way again."

"M'm."

At this unenthusiastic reponse, Paul Rannock glanced across the room at his son, who was standing with his back to him, looking out of the window, and persisted.

"I only remember her vaguely as a rather plain, shy little shrimp of a child. You saw a lot more of her, of course."

"Nice child. Sensitive, but with an unexpected capacity for digging her heels in. She saw us in an idealistic way. Can't think why."

"An expressive face. And an intelligent one. Far more interesting than mere prettiness."

"I've just time before lunch to go and stack up the logs I've done. I'll finish the job this afternoon," said Simon conclusively.

Paul Rannock returned to his papers as Simon left him. He would have liked to ask him more about the child, Sarah, but his son did not seem interested either in the child or the young woman whose visit had proved so warming. He wondered whether he had got over that Italian girl yet. It was nearly three years since that long, abortive love affair had come to an end, and although Simon never revealed his deepest feelings, the affair had, he thought, bitten deep. But it was always hard to know just what Simon was thinking. Perhaps his disapproval of this book project had colored his attitude toward Sarah Rushden. And if he was not in his son's confidence as much as he would wish, whose fault was that? Complete neglect for twenty-five of his son's thirty-one years hardly entitled him to his confidence now, when he had returned, broken in health, most of his money exhausted, to his son's care. He was fortunate to have Simon's good will. Grasping, beyond all merit, to ask for more. But he would like to see him happier.

Had he been able to read his son's thoughts just then as he stacked up the logs, they might have surprised him although they would have brought little comfort.

It had been an odd experience, Simon was thinking, going back to Rylands last night. So much of their school holidays had been spent there. The kindliness of Mrs. Rushden, and Mr. Rushden's warm interest in each of them had created at Rylands an atmosphere which drew them like a beacon from the cold misery of their own home, where his mother's chronic ill health and complaining nature coupled with the grudging service of a series of incompetent housekeepers cast a shadow over their lives, which chilled him even now whenever he entered this house.

Mr. Rushden had a natural sympathy with children and a gift for imparting his enthusiasms to them. He had been a teacher of English at Dilford Grammar School, and had been a great naturalist, too. It had been Mr. Rushden who had drawn him to Rylands rather than any wish for Sarah as a playmate, for the gap in their ages had relegated her to being yet another charge on his hands as well as Alison, Brian, and Katie. A charge he had found a little tedious at the end, when adolescence had its own problems, and he wanted companions of his own age. But Rylands and Sarah's grandparents still remained warm in his memory like a fire on a gray winter's day.

His mind ranging back to those days, odd little pictures of Sarah emerged. An expression of wonder on her face as she watched a spider spinning a web in the hedgerow along the lane one day. They could not get her to leave it, and she had come toiling up after them long afterward, just as he was getting exasperated and a little anxious, for she had only been about six years old then. "Plain," his father had said. Perhaps. A slightly snub nose, big brown eyes, thick brown hair cut in a page boy bob, and gaps in her teeth at the front. A small, thin child. He had scarcely recognized her last night in the young woman of fair height, slender, with hair caught back at the nape of her neck. Unremarkable features, but an expressive face, as his father had remarked. Always had been.

As though looking through an old album of snapshots, he recalled the face of the child Sarah enraptured by something she saw, dreamy and apart from them all; set and stubborn; or, saying goodbye at the end of the holidays, unbelievably forlorn. He remembered her hanging over the gate one cold, windy day at the end of the Easter holiday waving goodbye to them as they walked away down the lane. Only by chance had he glanced back to watch the flight of a heron down the river valley and caught sight of her in the distance still hanging over the gate watching them. She had waved her handkerchief again, a small dot in the distance. She must have been terribly sad.

And then it had all broken up. Mrs. Rushden died, Mr. Rushden disappeared, and Rylands became a neglected cottage inhabited by old Mrs. Lane. And the memories became dim, overlaid with the leaves of time, until now Sarah Rushden had returned to scuffle them up again. Better, perhaps, to have left them hidden. In the harsh light of maturity, they could lose some of their charm.

CHAPTER FOUR

SARAH HAD ACQUIRED a small black cat with pale green eyes. A strange piping sound outside the window one dark evening of drizzle and wind had called for investigation. On opening the front door, the cat had trotted in, headed straight for the sitting room fire, and set about restoring his ruffled fur. Inquiries in the neighborhood elicited no claimant, and even if one had been forthcoming, Sarah doubted whether it would have made any difference since Piper, as she named him, had obviously decided that Rylands was to his liking, and Piper's decisions were irreversible.

"Probably one of the cats from Seale Farm. They've got so many up there, they'd never notice if one was missing," said Mrs. Murcia, polishing the table with such vigor that her stout body shook like a jelly.

Mrs. Murcia, like Piper, had more or less wished herself on the scene. Meeting Sarah at the gates of Rylands one morning a few weeks after her arrival, she had waylaid her, dumping her shopping basket at her feet like an anchor.

"I'm Mrs. Murcia from the cottage next to the store," she announced baldly. "And you're Sarah Rushden. We missed your grandfather when he went abroad. Well-loved by everybody round here, he was."

Sarah smiled politely and said that she had missed him, too.

"Sad, him being left alone. Always so devoted, the two of them. But that's life. The best go. The ones we could well do without make the oldest bones," said Mrs. Murcia darkly.

There was a brooding look on her face that made Sarah wonder whose old bones she had in mind. She was short and round, with a ruddy complexion, bright blue eyes, and mousy hair which hung straight and wispy under a round felt hat. Sarah guessed her to be in her fifties.

"I used to come in here one morning a week to do a bit of cleaning for old Mrs. Lane. Jeff, my husband, used to work in the vegetable garden and the greenhouse. Wondered whether you might like the same arrangement. Of course, you're young and able to do for yourself, but I did hear that you were aiming to write a book, as well as helping Mr. Rannock up at Marlyn Manor, so perhaps you can do with a hand here."

"I hadn't exactly budgeted for it, although I could do with more time for my writing."

"No need to worry about terms. We can work something out, I'm sure. If we could have any spare produce from the vegetable garden, that would be a fair bargain, I reckon. We sell what we don't want ourselves to Jim Roberts's store. Fetches a fair price these days. That was the arrangement we had with Mrs. Lane."

And that was the arrangement which she obviously expected to have with Miss Rushden.

"Well, I'm only a novice gardener, although I'm keen," said Sarah. "I shall have my hands full with the rest of the garden, so I'd be happy to leave the vegetable garden and greenhouse to an experienced hand."

"Can't beat Jeff. He grows the best vegetables for miles around. Started life as a gardener. Couldn't make a living. Became a postman, and spare-time gardener. He retired from the post last year. He'll keep you supplied with the best vegetables you've ever tasted. No artificial fertilizers. All organic stuff. That's his creed."

Mrs. Murcia proceeded to enlarge on the horticultural skills of Jeff Murcia to such an extent that when Sarah met him for the first time, it seemed something of a let-down, for the small, wizened, sad-looking man did not suggest a performer of miracles in any sphere, but when she walked down the garden with him to the large vegetable garden behind the golden privet hedge, a fanatical light sprang up in his dark eyes as he surveyed it.

"I left it in good order in August. As soon as she knew you were going to inherit the cottage, she refused to have me here. We'd never got on too well, mind you. Cantankerous and ignorant about gardening, she was. Threatened to have me up for trespassing when I tried to carry on regardless. Now look at it. And I'd come to rely on it for a bit of income. A proper mess. I must get to work."

And so the Murcias as well as Piper moved in on her life, and Sarah found that they suited her very well.

As Christmas drew near, she was well pleased with the way her new life was shaping. She had done all she could afford to rehabilitate the cottage, was making good progress in clearing up the garden and planning for the spring, had roughed out the characters and plot of her book, and had settled into an agreeable working routine at Marlyn Manor. And if sometimes in the evenings she thought of Nick with an ache in her heart, there was always Piper at her feet, gazing into the fire, ready to purr at the touch of her finger, and the characters of her book ready to spring to life in her imagination and keep her company.

She was presiding over the dying stages of a bonfire at the end of the garden one cold Saturday afternoon when Simon turned up.

"That's welcome," he said holding his hands to the glowing embers. "A frost tonight, I think."

"Good for breaking up the soil, according to Jeff."

"You look very workmanlike," he said, eyeing her navy windbreaker, slacks, and Wellington boots.

It was a change, she thought, for him to notice her as a person at all. On the few occasions they had met since that first encounter, he had seemed so detached as to make her feel invisible. She threw on the last of the pile of twigs and rubbish and leaned on her rake, gazing into the rekindled flames. They surged and flared for a few moments, then died down into a steady glow again. It was nearly dark, and the fire seemed to hold them in a warm clasp against the encroaching cold darkness of the garden.

"There's a strange primeval satisfaction in a bonfire," she said, putting her rake aside and sitting down on a convenient tree stump.

Simon was leaning against a hazel tree looking up at the moon through the bare branches. The embers of the fire twinkled in the gentle eddies of air, now glowing fiercely, now subsiding. There was no need to watch it any longer for safety's sake, but Sarah sat on, seeing pictures in the fire, warm and at peace. A peace which Simon did not disturb. It was a completely harmonious silence that wrapped them round, and it was not broken until an owl hooting nearby brought Sarah's eyes away from the fire to find Simon studying her. In the half-light of the fire it was not easy to see his expression, but his voice was gentle as he said, "A child of nature. Captivated."

"Sorry. I was lost."

"No need to be sorry. An enviable state. And you haven't even wondered why I've come uninvited into your retreat."

"No Rannock needs an invitation here. They have a passport."

"For old times' sake," he said, his voice gently teasing as he sat down on the stump beside her and put a friendly hand on her shoulder.

"Exactly."

"Nice, loyal Sarah. I came to ask you if you would spend Christmas with us. Alison and I are trying to arrange a family reunion for the old man. The first, believe it or not, since he came home five years ago. He asked for it with such diffidence that we thought we ought to make an effort to round up Katie and Brian. We'd like you to join us. Will you?"

"I'd love to. I've been hoping to see Alison and Brian and Katie again."

"Splendid. Can't guarantee that we'll get the two young ones here, but Alison is nothing if not persistent, and I shall leave the spade work to her."

The cold of the garden was beginning to gain on the warmth of the dying fire, and they walked back to the cottage together. It seemed natural, then, for Simon to stay and have tea. She found him a handy man about the place, for he replenished her log basket and wielded a bread knife with great precision. Between them, they accounted for hardboiled eggs, a large plate of bread and butter, scones and blackberry jelly, and a good wedge of the fruitcake.

"Mrs. Murcia's," confessed Sarah in reply to his compliments on the cake. "She brought it along yesterday. My cooking is rather a hit and miss affair at present. I've not had much experience. I ate most of my meals out when I lived in London or else existed on eggs in various guises and cheese salads. I get much hungrier here, though."

"You're happy here, aren't you?"

"Very."

"Don't miss London?"

"Urban life is such an unnatural life. At least for me. Here, I'm at home. The local people have all proved so friendly, too. On account of my grandparents, as far as the older inhabitants are concerned. They're still remembered with affection."

"Yes. They radiated their own warmth and stability. Upholders of the old values. We were too young to realize it at the time, of course, but looking back, you appreciate it."

They cleared away and washed up, then sat by the fire in an idle mood.

"Ought I to go?" Simon asked quizzically at one point.

"Not unless you want to."

"I feel very comfortable and disgustingly lazy after all that tea. It's years since I had a farmhouse tea. You're spinning a web of old customs round me. The simple life. I'd forgotten what it was like."

Encouraged by his relaxed mood, Sarah said, "Has life been so very complex for you?"

"Not more so than for most other people, I guess. Complex isn't quite the word. Distorted, perhaps, by responsibilities I never wanted."

"The family. Tell me about it, Simon. Although I knew you all so well when I was a child, I never learned anything about your home life. Never saw your mother or set foot in your home."

"It wasn't a home. My mother was a chronic invalid. How much of it was physical and how much psychological is hard to say. We were looked after by a whole string of housekeepers when we were young. Looked after is overstating it. We were fed, and the house was kept in some sort of order. Money wasn't plentiful, and it grew scarcer as we grew older. Alison escaped by marriage; Katie and Brian left home as soon as they could get jobs and support themselves."

"When did your mother die?"

"Six years ago. My father came home six months later. We couldn't find him to tell him the news. He was lost in some remote part of Africa. We wanted to sell the house, which was heavily mortgaged, but couldn't while my father was out of reach. We'd just decided to try to let it when he turned up. He'd bitten off more than he'd bargained for in his last venture. Been captured by some tribesmen and narrowly escaped with his life after being tortured. Physically and mentally, he was a wreck. How he got himself home, I'll never know. That's why I didn't want him to embark on these memoirs. For a time it was touch and go whether his mind would recover from the shock. I didn't want him to relive any of it again. But so far, it doesn't seem to be affecting him adversely. In fact, since you appeared, he's seemed brighter than I've known him for the past five years."

"I'm glad you've told me. A burdensome life for you, Simon. I'm sorry. Was there nobody outside the family to console you?"

"Partially, perhaps. But that's another story. And quite enough of my affairs. This cottage," he added, looking around the quiet, firelit room, "saw our happiest times."

"For me, too."

"Nobody to console you since then, as you so tactfully put it?"

"And I won't be as evasive as you. I've had one good friend. He's not interested in being anything more, though."

"Would you have liked him to be?"

"Yes."

"His loss. You're a born homemaker. I don't think it's stricken you too hard, though, has it? You seem so happy with your lot now."

"I have a taste for solitude. And I love writing. Also, I'm a little wary of marriage after the example of my parents."

"You could just as easily cite your grandparents for the opposite argument. You're not expecting me to eat chestnuts after that tea, are you?"

"I thought I'd do a few while the fire's glowing."

"Tell me more about this book of yours. I do believe my father's more interested in it than in his own."

They chatted on about books and writing, keeping off personal matters, until he rose to go, when he said with a simplicity that touched her, "Thank you for letting me share your retreat, Sarah. I'd forgotten what it was like, to be at peace."

Under the hall light, the deep lines around his eyes and mouth which aged him beyond his years seemed more marked than ever, giving a haggard cast to his lean face, which suggested that the outline of the past that he had given her hid far deeper stresses and strains than his brief words had revealed.

"Come whenever you like. It's good for you to relax," she said gently.

"Goodnight," he said, and kissed her. He turned and waved a hand at the gate, then was gone, his footsteps echoing down the lane in the quiet of the frosty night.

Piper shot by her with an affronted air and made straight for the fire. His feet were cold, and he had been kept waiting. But, settled in front of the fire, paws tucked neatly under him, he gazed at the dying flames of the fire and purred and purred.

CHAPTER FIVE

SARAH MET THE second of her childhood friends two days before Christmas. She was editing the first chapter of Paul Rannock's memoirs when she heard a car draw up. She knew that Alison was due that day to help the housekeeper make preparations for the holiday. The room in which she worked was one which led out of Paul Rannock's study, and she heard only muted sounds of the arrival while she went on with her work, but it was difficult to concentrate as her mind kept wandering to Alison, wondering whether she, like Simon, would be hard to link with the child of all those years ago.

And then, a little later, her door opened and a voice said, "Can I come in? Father says pack up your work now until after Christmas, and come and have tea with us. I'm Alison. Remember?"

"Of course. As if I'd forgotten any of you. It's good to see you again."

Alison, at twenty-seven, had a sturdily built figure, wore her fair straight hair swept up in a severe style, which nevertheless suited her regular features and calm expression, and created an impression of maturity beyond her years. She studied Sarah with friendly curiosity.

"Odd, our paths crossing again like this. Those were happy days we spent at Rylands with you when we were kids. Your grandparents were so kind." She paused for a moment, a soft look in her eyes as she remembered, then went on briskly, "Simon says you get on very well with my father, which is quite an achievement."

"I don't find him difficult."

"We, Simon and I, weren't too keen on this book about his explorations, but he seems to be better for the effort. Anyway, I'm glad you're going to be here for Christmas. It'll ease things. A grisly idea, this family reunion, but we must try to make a go of it."

"Is it so grisly?"

"We all hate this house. I wanted Father to let me have the reunion in my home, but he says he's not up to leaving here now. Typical excuse for having his own way, as always."

It was not said with any resentment, rather a calm statement of fact.

"When are Brian and Katie coming? I'm looking forward to seeing them again."

"On Christmas morning, in time to avoid the chores," she said with a wry smile.

"Mrs. Pilsen?"

"She's off tomorrow to spend Christmas with her daughter in Kent. Can't say I'm sorry. I'd sooner do the chores on my own than bear her permanent air of injury. Just because my father has never entertained here before is no reason why he shouldn't. It's his home, after all. Hardly an asset to the Christmas spirit, Mrs. Pilsen."

"No. The wind is always chilly from that quarter. Can I help you tomorrow? I'd be glad to."

"Bless you, another pair of hands would be welcome. I want to make it as festive as possible for Debbie's sake. At five years old, Christmas means so much. Come along and meet my daughter and my husband. Don had some leave due, so he's added it on to Christmas and will be able to look after Debbie while I try to organize some festivities in this house of blight."

"On leave? Is he in the service?"

"Civil Service," said Alison briefly as Sarah finished tidying her desk and followed her to the sitting room.

An uneasy silence seemed to be reigning there, and the dark-haired little girl sitting sedately on a stool by her grandfather's chair and the man in the armchair opposite both heralded Alison's reappearance with smiles of relief. Deborah had her mother's pale blue eyes, but the heart-shaped face framed by the straight page boy bob had a quirky charm that reminded Sarah briefly of Brian as the child smiled shyly at her. She bore no resemblance at all to her father, who was a slight, rather short, sandy-haired man with neat features dominated by heavy horn-rimmed spectacles. He greeted Sarah affably and then retired into silence, allowing Alison to dispense tea from the cart and dominate the conversation, which she did with a quiet authority, making Sarah feel that she was back at school again.

Paul Rannock had retired into his shell. The little girl was obviously nervous of him and kept stealing glances at his disfigured face. If he was aware of it, he made no attempt to reassure the child. Sarah suspected that in Alison's presence he was more than usually weighed down by guilt. It was with some relief that she took her leave soon after and walked home down the lane.

It was a mild night, with a crescent moon playing hide and seek among thin, drifting clouds. The lights from the scattered cottages of the hamlet shone out with a friendly message in the darkness, and the windows of the general store, framed with tinsel and full of gaily decorated boxes and jars of Christmas goods, were colorful enough to please all eyes except those of Scrooge. The inn close by had sported a Christmas tree at the entrance, whose baubles and colored lights added yet another cheerful note. Then the lane closed in on her and she was alone with the dark night until the white wicket gate of Rylands loomed up palely. Jeff Murcia had been working in the vegetable garden that afternoon and had switched on the porch light when he left, presumably to illuminate the flower pot full of the Brussels sprouts he had picked for her evening meal. Piper appeared from nowhere and came to meet her, rubbing round her legs and uttering his peculiar piping greeting. After the bleakness of Marlyn Manor, her own small cottage seemed to welcome her all the more warmly.

Reporting for duty at Marlyn Manor the next morning, Sarah was dispatched to the village with a long shopping list made out by Alison, who wanted to supplement the more solid fare already prepared by the housekeeper with trifles, jellies, sweets, and shortbread, all of which she proposed to make that day.

"Don's digestion will never stand up to Mrs. Pilsen's Christmas pudding and mince pies, and they're not suitable for Debbie, anyway," said Alison firmly. "Would you like Don to drive you? He's taken Debbie out for a walk but he'll be back soon."

"Not necessary, thanks. It's only a couple of miles to the village and I'll go on my bicycle. It has large carrying bags that will hold all we want."

Her shopping duties discharged, she was asked to raid the garden that afternoon for anything to decorate the house.

"It looks such a morgue. If you'll take over the house, I'll be able to finish the cooking and decorate the little Christmas tree we brought with us."

And so Sarah found herself in the jungle of Marlyn Manor's garden. With the deciduous trees all bare now, it did not look quite so dark and forbidding, but apart from a few straggling pink chrysanthemums surviving among the tangled wreckage of one of the borders, there seemed little of a decorative nature. She picked some laurel and ivy and then searched the old holly tree in the thicket for some berries. There were a few near the top.

A holly tree not being the most suitable of trees for climbing, she went in search of a ladder in the garden shed. Her luck was in, for hidden in a dark corner among a jumble of wheelbarrows, rusty garden implements, wire netting, and other impedimenta, she found a rickety, wooden stepladder. It creaked ominously as she cautiously climbed to the top step and balanced herself by holding on with one hand to the overhanging bough of an oak tree while with the other she wielded her shears, letting the pieces of holly fall to the ground.

The piece with the most berries remained perversely just out of reach. She was about to try to stretch her arm another inch toward it, when Simon's voice said, "Leave that to me. We don't want you in a wheelchair for Christmas."

She turned around cautiously and smiled down at him.

"Hullo, Simon. I'm glad you're here. Alison can do with another recruit."

"I bet she can. Look out!"

The ladder swayed perilously, and Simon caught her round the waist and swung her off as it collapsed, the frayed rope between the steps and the support having broken.

"Well, it lasted just long enough," she said, a little breathless, as she looked up at his dark face.

"A Merry Christmas, Sarah," he said. "If I need an excuse, there's some mistletoe up there."

He kissed her and smiled down at her startled face.

"Where? The mistletoe. I looked everywhere for some."

"There's a bunch on the top fork of that oak."

She screwed her head round and peered up.

"So there is. I never spotted it."

"Wouldn't have made any difference if you had. You'd need a helicopter to pick it."

"I don't know. It's not such a difficult tree to climb. You'd have done it once."

"But I don't need to now, do I?" he said, and kissed her again before swinging her to her feet.

"You're in a very frisky mood."

"Not really. You have a very kissable mouth. If you'll come out here at intervals and stand under the mistletoe, it will go far to helping me get through this Christmas."

"Are you used to a diet of kisses, then?" she asked lightly, as she stooped to gather up her pieces of holly.

"No. But lollipops under the mistletoe are permissible and harmless, don't you agree?"

"When the parties are compatible, yes."

"And in this case they are, I think, don't you? It's all this *auld lang syne* aura that surrounds us."

She laughed, suddenly liking him enormously.

"As you say. And I don't see why you're so pessimistic about Christmas. It will warm up, I'm sure."

"Let's hope so. My father's trying hard, but it's pathetic, really, you know. You can't wipe out the past. Pretend it never happened. It's become part of all of us. We're strangers to him. We never knew him. How can we be transformed into a loving family at this late stage to ease his conscience?"

"You can try. And you're not a stranger to him."

"Not to the wreck of a man who returned out of the blue five years ago, because I had to help him, and I feel sorry for him. Who wouldn't, seeing him now? But I don't know him as my father. We never had one. Only a legendary one, the object of my mother's complaints. It's no use turning sentimental at the end of your life. The damage has been done. We can't make a cozy picture for him now any more than you can transform Marlyn Manor with those bits of evergreen and poor little chrysanthemums."

His mood had changed to the harsh bitterness that had repelled her at their first meeting.

"Sometimes," she said, "it is necessary to pretend, and sometimes the pretense becomes true."

"Thank you for helping, anyway. Your old loyalties can be costly, though, Sarah."

"Not so far," she said firmly. "Can you help me with these decorations? Your long reach will be useful."

"If that arch organizer, my sister, hasn't already got other duties lined up for me, I'll help you with pleasure. I'm good at holding ladders firm and rather take to the job."

"The idea was that you should be the one up the ladder."

"Don't know that I'll find that so agreeable," he said, as he followed her into the house.

By concentrating their efforts on the diningroom and sitting room, they did manage to soften the aspect of those large, high-ceilinged rooms with their heavy, dark oak furniture and drab carpets.

"I've some Christmas roses out in my garden. I'll bring them tomorrow and put them on the chest in the hall," said Sarah, putting the last pieces of laurel in the bowl to fill out the chrysanthemums and placing it on the oak refectory table.

"Let's hope the weather stays mild. This house is never warm at the best of times. I'd better fill that log basket," said Simon.

Having existed on scratch meals that day, they found themselves hungry in the evening after their labors, and Sarah cut sandwiches in the kitchen with Donald Marshfield deputized by his wife to assist her. A little tired, Sarah found his precise manner niggling and wished he would leave her to her task. He could not relax his formal politeness, it seemed, but wore it like a bowler hat.

"Don't you think . . . a little too fat? Allow me," he said, moving the sliced ham delicately from its paper on to a dish and meticulously trimming all the fat from the edges.

Some people, thought Sarah darkly, as she sliced some tomatoes, might like a little fat.

"No brown bread?" he asked with a polite little smile as Sarah wielded the bread knife on a white loaf.

"There is a brown loaf, but it's very fresh and difficult to cut thin."

"So much better for you than white, you know. Shall I do a few brown ones when you've finished the white? I'm rather good at cutting thin bread. You ask Alison."

He was also rather good at removing the skin from the tomatoes she had sliced, while indicating gently that it would have been easier to have removed it before slicing them.

"By putting them in boiling water for a minute," said Sarah swiftly before he could enlighten her with a kindly smile. "I didn't think it necessary if I sliced them thinly. Some roughage is good for you, you know."

"A little indigestible for me, I'm afraid."

Sarah handed him the bread knife with her sweetest smile, saying, "Over to you for the brown ones."

She had hoped that the blunt knife and the new bread might defeat his high standards, but although frowning at the inadequacy of the knife, by a patient and steady sawing movement, he did indeed succeed in cutting thin, regular slices.

Watching his intent face and small deft fingers,

Sarah wondered what it was in him that had attracted Alison. In looks, he was oddly negative, and only his heavy horn-rimmed spectacles would have enabled one to pick him out from a crowd. His personality was equally blank, no emotions emerging from that bland covering. Perhaps there were no emotions to emerge. She could imagine his desk in his office, with everything in its place down to the last paperclip. Alison must have discovered something hidden from the rest of the world, she thought, as she turned her attention to the coffee. Happily, there was only one way of making coffee in a percolator.

Paul Rannock, who looked drawn and tired, declined the sandwiches and substituted a whisky and soda for coffee. When they had finished, he stood up and said, "I'm off to bed, but before I go, Sarah, there's something in my study I want to show you."

In his study, he drew a folder from a drawer in his desk and passed her the drawing it contained.

"Finished it last night. Been trying to get hold of you all day, but you've been as elusive as a moth. Like it?"

She studied it with delighted surprise. It was a drawing of a girl rolling a hoop along a pavement, her pigtail bobbing against her coat, a tam perched on her head, one gloved hand wielding the hoop stick. She was running past the railings and gate of a house, an old-fashioned lamppost ahead of her. There were some leaves flying past her, and the sense of movement which he had captured in the figure of the running child was so real that Sarah could feel the wind on her own face as she looked at it. So that was why he had asked to see the first pages of her book.

"My Laura!" she exclaimed delightedly. "You've caught her exactly. I must be a better writer than I thought for you to have matched my imaginary picture so accurately. I never knew you were an artist," she added, for this drawing was no amateur effort.

"I had some training when I was young. Thought of it as a career until I was bitten by the travel bug. I've done a bit on and off."

"The period's all there."

"Only had to dig back to my own childhood memories."

"Illustrations like this would be marvelous for the book. I know my publisher would be delighted. Would you be willing?"

"Nothing would please me more. I thoroughly enjoyed that escape into the past."

"I'll discuss it with Mr. Birch—he's my publisher—after Christmas and show him this. I can't tell you how thrilled I am by it. This could be the start of a splendid collaboration. If you're sure it won't tire you, with your own book to cope with as well."

"Oh that! Drawing will be a refreshing escape to your happier, simpler world. I'm glad you like my effort."

"The best Christmas present I could have had, discovering your talent and finding you so much on my wavelength where my writing is concerned. You'll make the book a success in spite of any shortcomings of mine, I'm sure. You must share in the rewards, of course."

"Now the boot's on the other foot. You can say this is in payment of services rendered by you if you want to, but in reality you will have provided me with a delightful hobby. Now, my dear, I'm for bed. Must hoard my strength for the rest of Christmas. You'll be here tomorrow and day after, won't you?"

"Yes. I'm coming over each day."

"Splendid. I like to have you about the place. You reassure me, Sarah. I've reason to be grateful to the Rushdens. First, dear old Martin, and now you. Perhaps my only two real friends. But then I've always been a solitary creature. Not so good at this end of one's life, though. Goodnight, my dear. Thank you."

He laid a hand on her shoulder for a moment, then gave her his painful, twisted smile and went.

Simon was alone in the sitting room. Alison and Donald had gone to fill Deborah's Christmas stocking and hang it by the fireplace. Amused by the mental picture of Donald filling a Christmas stocking with geometrical precision, Sarah showed Simon the drawing with happy, excited eyes.

"Yes, he is gifted. He was beginning to gain some recognition, I believe, when his itch to explore took over."

"Chimborazo, Cotopaxi,
They had stolen my soul away!"
quoted Sarah, thinking that it was perhaps a pity that Paul Rannock had not cultivated his artistic talent instead.

"I remember hearing that poem read when I was at school, and I thought then of my father. It certainly applied to him. An obsession with unknown country, primitive tribes, overriding everything. Anyway, an unexpectedly fruitful partnership seems to have sprung up between you two. I'm glad. A couple of romantics, so perhaps it's not quite so odd as it looks."

"Time I went. It's been quite a day."

"I'll walk home with you."

"No need. I've got my bicycle. I used it to go to the village for some shopping this morning."

When he fetched the bicycle from the shed where she had stored it, fearing rain, he said they should walk it.

"You can't cycle without lights."

"There's seldom any traffic in the lane at night."

"On Christmas Eve there could well be some. I hope you don't make a habit of cycling at night on this."

"No. I never use it after dark. Only to cycle to the

village when our general store can't supply me with what I want."

"It's a decrepit old iron. Needs oiling," he said as he wheeled it down the drive. "And the brakes aren't exactly efficient," he added, testing them.

"Don't fuss. You're as bad as Donald."

"There's fussing and fussing. I must confess to finding Donald a bit of a trial myself. When it comes to risking your neck on a bicycle without lights in a dark lane, though, I can fuss as well as anyone. I'm a motorist, remember. Where did you get this old crate from, anyway?"

"Mrs. Murcia knew somebody who knew somebody whose daughter didn't want it any more. So a small sum provided me with transport to the village when necessary. What a lovely night! All balmy and peaceful."

Two cars, in fact, passed them in the lane, but Simon forebore to comment and seemed withdrawn. Sarah, enthusing about the magic feeling of Christmas Eve in the country, evoked only a brief response and fell silent as they neared the cottage. He handed the bicycle over to her at the gate.

"Goodnight, Sarah. Thanks for your help today. And get those brakes seen to," he added, as he turned away, and in a few moments he was swallowed up in the dark tunnel of the lane.

She felt a little blank as she put her bicycle away, disappointed that he could not share her mood of delight in the peace of the night and the special quality of Christmas Eve. Foolish, romantic Sarah, he would think. She was never quite sure about how he felt toward her. Sometimes they would be in complete harmony, easy with each other, at peace. At others, he made her feel, as he had that night, like the child Sarah, who had to be seen safely home, an added duty. And at others still, he became a harsh and almost frightening stranger. And she acknowledged to herself for the first time that night, as she paused in the porch to take a last look at the night sky, that what Simon Rannock felt about her was beginning to matter.

CHAPTER SIX

AT THE SOUND of the car, Sarah looked up from the table, which she was setting for lunch, and went to the diningroom window. Alison came in from the kitchen just then and joined her.

"It's Brian. And he's brought a girl with him. How like him, without telling me! That'll mean another place, Sarah."

The tall, fair man and dark, pants-suited girl disappeared into the entrance and the bell rang. Sarah went with Alison into the hall, where Paul Rannock was limping to the door.

"My dear boy, it's good to see you!" he said.

"Hello, Dad. Brought Joan with me. Peach of a girl. Know you'll like her ... Alison, dear girl, Merry Christmas ... The old place doesn't seem to have changed."

His ready babble of speech stopped while his father introduced Sarah, but flowed on easily to embrace her.

"Little Sarah Rushden ... My pet ... Played together when we were young and innocent, Joan ... How's the family, Alison? Still only one?"

He spoke, thought Sarah, like a cheerleader at a holiday camp. She had not been his pet. In fact, they had often quarrelled when she had found his teasing too much for her. Now his teasing seemed to have turned into an all-embracing *bonhomie* which she felt struck a false note. His companion was a tall, pleasant-looking young woman, content to leave the talking to Brian for the time being. It occurred to

Sarah that he was uneasy about this meeting with his father and was using Joan and his own ready tongue for shields. She knew that he had only seen his father once since his return to England.

Alison drew Brian back as Paul Rannock ushered them into the sitting room for drinks.

"Is she staying the night?" she whispered.

"Of course. Can't expect the girl to go back to London on her own. Unless I'm allowed to go back with her," he added with a smile.

"No. You must stay until tomorrow. I just wanted to know whether I had another room to make ready."

"I knew there'd be no difficulty in this barn of a place. Don't worry, Alison. Where's the worthy Donald and the offspring?"

"Out for a walk with Simon. I must get things organized."

Alison ran upstairs and Brian lifted his eyebrows and smiled in a conspiratorial fashion at Sarah.

"Busy as a bee, our Alison, as always. She'd be miserable if she hadn't anything to cope with. I remember so well your big brown eyes, Sarah. Come and tell me all about yourself."

Looking up at his smiling, good-looking face, she could not equate him with the boy. He had been a thin little lad with sharp, regular features and a quirky liveliness. Now a sleek expansiveness had filled out and blurred that old picture. He was wearing a check sports jacket over a polo-necked, canary-colored sweater. Somehow, he didn't fit in with Marlyn Manor and the past at all.

While she sat, a glass of sherry in her hand, and told him a little of her life, she felt that his attention was only partially given to her although he appeared attentive. Now and again his eyes strayed to his father, who was talking politely to Joan. When Simon, Donald, and Debbie came in, she made an excuse and slipped away to complete setting the dining table.

When the youngest member of the Rannock family arrived, however, Sarah was forced to rearrange the place settings once again and add a small square table from the hall to the refectory dining table, for Katie arrived with no fewer than four people in train.

When in after years Sarah remembered that Christmas, and it was one she never forgot, it was always the picture of Katie's arrival which sprang first to mind for its dynamic effect. It was as if an electric shock had passed through them.

She burst into that dark, gaunt hall looking radiant in a cherry-red coat, her black hair caught in thick curls at the nape of her neck, laughing behind a pile of gaily wrapped parcels. The two men behind her carried a hamper between them, and the two women bringing up the rear each bore a bottle wrapped in colored paper.

Sarah, standing apart half hidden by the grandfather clock, watched the impact of this retinue on the rest of the family with some amusement, her heart warming immediately to the gay vitality and beauty of Katie. Embracing her father quickly, she included her brothers and sister in a general greeting and went on,

"I knew you'd all be pleased to have some lovely people for Christmas. We've brought some vittles and goodies so that we shan't be putting a strain on the supplies, Alison. This is my friend Max, who is also my leading man. And Sally and Jim. Poor dears. The most awful thing happened to them yesterday. Their flat was ransacked. Food, drink, jewelry and even clothes stolen. I said they simply must put it out of their minds and get right away for Christmas. Wasn't it awful, on Christmas Eve? Jim's our producer and Sally's an angel and mothers us all. And now, my biggest surprise for you, Simon. Anna Pirano," concluded Katie, as though introducing royalty.

Sarah's eyes had been registering Paul Rannock's bewilderment, Alison's look of incredulity, which had given way to a tight-lipped expression not suggestive of Christmas good will, and a certain conspiratorial air about Brian, but she was brought up short by Simon's frozen expression as the tall, dark girl Katie called Anna came into the hall and looked at him expectantly. He had gone quite white and a curious rigidity seemed to grip him. Then he relaxed and a polite mask wiped out all expression on his face as he said calmly, "A very big surprise indeed, Katie. How did you conjure Anna out of Italy?"

Katie's dark gray eyes looked at him as though puzzled and disappointed at his reaction; then she smiled and said, "I'll leave that to Anna to explain. And this must be Debbie. What a big girl you are now," she said, stooping to the child who had been hiding behind her mother and giving her a hug. "And where's Sarah? I'm longing to meet Sarah again. You said she would be here, Alison."

Sarah emerged and had both hands taken in a warm clasp as Katie said, "I didn't see you. This hall is so dark."

"And you're short-sighted, Katie," said Brian. "You should wear your glasses."

She made a face at him and said, "It's delightful to have you back in our family circle again, Sarah. Not that I have any but rather vague memories about those holidays when we were children, but such as they are, they're all happy ones. And you were the center of them. We'll have a long talk about them. A Christmas of reunions. Exciting, isn't it?"

But the man who had planned this family reunion so that he could get to know his children better and try to reach an understanding with them had not envisaged a party like this, and as they bustled around him fetching in cases, laughing, and chatting with each other, he limped back to his chair by the fire in the sitting room, looking old and tired and disheartened.

Although Marlyn Manor had a generous endowment of rooms, it did not stretch to accommodation for all the visitors who had come. However Alison shifted them round, they were a room short.

"Oh, it's only for one night," said Katie airily, drawn into the kitchen by Alison and Sarah for a discussion of ways and means. "You can use the couch in the sitting room for Brian, or I dare say Simon won't mind vacating a room and driving back to his flat at Dilford tonight. It's not far, after all. Perhaps he'd like to take Anna with him," she added mischievously.

Alison, however, was in no mood for levity. With eyes blazing, her quiet composure utterly routed, she closed the kitchen door against any eavesdroppers and turned on her young sister.

"You're the absolute limit, Katie. Father wanted a quiet reunion with us, and you bring down this horde of strangers."

"Not exactly a horde. Three strangers and one old friend of Simon."

"And how could you be so cruel as to spring that on him? Knowing what that girl put him through."

"But she's free now. The situation's changed."

"I don't care what's changed. You had no right to do it. Thoughtless and utterly selfish of you. As if it wasn't enough having a stranger arrive with Brian. I haven't prepared for a party like this, and it's quite unsuitable for a man in Father's state of health."

Katie's eyes were sparkling now as she returned the attack.

"And if you thought Brian and I were going to

endure a quiet family Christmas in this morgue with a man who calls himself our father but whom we never saw for years on end, who left his invalid wife to the care of his children . . ."

"To Simon and me. You and Brian got out quickly enough."

"Who used up on foreign exploration all the money he'd inherited," went on Katie ignoring the interruption, "who robbed us of any chance of happiness when we were children and went his own way, and who's come back a wreck to be a burden on Simon . . ."

"You and Brian," interrupted Alison again. "Did you get together on this, then?"

"We decided that we'd got to bring some life into the place. We find Father embarrassing and painful. With a crowd, we thought we could get by, and so we can. We'll all chip in with the chores, if that's what's biting you."

"I know just how useful you'll all be," returned Alison bitingly. "I'd have thought you could have spared two days for the old man. He's not likely to see many more Christmases."

"Why should we?"

"Because he's sorry for past neglect and wants to make amends."

"It's a bit late, isn't it?"

"Yes," said Alison, quietly now and in control again. "It is a bit late. But if people ask forgiveness, Christmas is a bad time to refuse it."

"All right. I'm sorry, Alison, but you do lecture so. And Father gives me the horrors. He looks so . . . Well, how can we love him when he never loved us? He lived the life he wanted. Now we do the same. Anyway, company may cheer him up."

"Well, let's get back to ways and means," said Alison resignedly. "Where are we going to put your friends? I don't want Simon to give up his room and drive back to Dilford tonight. He's the only one of you whose help will be reliable. I need his support with Father."

"You've got Donald. He's well-trained to be helpful."

As Alison's eyes signaled danger again, Sarah broke in hastily.

"I've a spare room at my cottage. Perhaps Brian's friend, Joan, or Anna could have that."

"Let me," said Katie. "I'd love to see Rylands again. Can I, Sarah?"

"Of course," said Sarah, thinking that Katie ought to be spanked, but won over in spite of herself by the lovely smiling face, all anger now dispersed, claws sheathed, in a rapid change of mood which Sarah remembered now as characteristic of the child Katie.

"Angel! Now I'll go and sort the others out. You don't have to worry about them, Alison. They're all the easiest people in the world to get on with and they'll cheer things up in Bleak House no end, I promise. And aren't you curious about Anna?"

"No," snapped Alison. "Anna's created enough havoc in Simon's life. That's one guest we could well have done without."

"That may not be Simon's verdict."

"If I were you, I'd steer clear of Simon for a bit. He won't take kindly to your interference in his affairs, and he can be very effective when he's angry, as you well know. *And* you can't get round him as you get round most people."

"Anna was my friend before he met her. Anyway, I consider I'm doing him a good turn."

"Oh Katie! Have you no common sense?"

"Have you no sense of romance?"

"You'd better be off and show your friends to their rooms. Anna can have your old room. Next time you want to treat the house like a hotel, I'd like to have prior warning."

"Dear Alison. If only you didn't always have to have everything just so, these things wouldn't worry you. We're all used to making do. Touring makes you very adaptable. Just relax," concluded Katie, and gave them a delightful smile as she left them.

"Relax!" echoed Alison disgustedly. "Oh well, we must do the best we can. Katie's thoughtless and impulsive, but her attitude to Father is understandable, I suppose. And if anyone needed a father when she was young, it was Katie. She ran wild and there was nobody to check her." She turned as Simon came in, looking at him rather apprehensively.

"We shall need more glasses, Alison," he said. "Are there any stacked away here? I've exhausted the supply in the sideboard."

"There are some in the cupboard under the bookcase in Father's study. How is he taking all this?"

"Jollity not being his strong point, he has retired to a corner where he can survey the tribe. Nobody, so far, seems inclined to disturb him," said Simon with cold incisiveness.

Sarah, trimming more Brussels sprouts at the sink, could almost feel the east wind of his mood.

"Have you seen Debbie?" asked Alison.

"Donald was in the conservatory reading to her when I last saw him. He appears to prefer the potted palms to the company, and I can't say I blame him," said Simon, and went out in no mood, evidently, to discuss the situation.

Alison looked after him unhappily.

"Poor Simon," she said. "I could take a stick to Katie for this. How are you getting on, Sarah?"

"I don't think we'll have enough. I think I'd better dash home and get some more. Jeff left me with a good supply from the garden."

"Bless you! Don't know how I'd cope without you, Sarah. I must apologize for landing you with all these chores, though."

"Don't worry. I shall enjoy a breath of air. The turkey smells good."

"Yes. A good thing it's bigger than I expected. I know one thing," added Alison with unaccustomed bite. "I'm going to set Katie and Brian to do the washing up this afternoon if it's the last thing I do."

Out in the lane, the air was fresh and sweet, and a pale sunshine flickered through the overhanging branches of the trees as Sarah walked briskly to Rylands, reflecting on the events of the morning. Now her circle of Rannocks was complete, the memories of her childhood adjusted to the realities of the present. And uppermost in her mind was the question mark that hung over the newcomer, Anna Pirano, and Simon. Nobody had enlightened her. It was part of the past unknown to her. An unhappy part for Simon it seemed. This Christmas was turning out to be a strange mix-up. Only one thing was certain. It would not be dull.

CHAPTER SEVEN

PAUL RANNOCK, WHO had retired for a short rest after the noisy and hilarious Christmas lunch, descended the stairs slowly and cautiously and struggled into his overcoat in the hall. Sarah, emerging from the sitting room, smiled when she saw him.

"I was just thinking of doing the same. I don't know what that wine was that Katie's friends brought, but after making me feel like a soaring lark, I've come down to earth with a jarring thud. It doesn't seem to have affected the others like that," she added, as a lively rendering of a song from a popular musical show reached a crescendo in the sitting room.

"Have a turn round the garden with me, then, my dear."

They walked as far as the thicket and sat down on the wooden seat there. Paul Rannock fished in his pocket and pulled out a book.

"Haven't done anything about Christmas presents. I'm not able to get about even if I knew what to buy. But I'd like you to have this book of poems by W. H. Davies which your grandfather gave me and which somehow seems so much in tune with you, Sarah. The same gentle simplicity and kinship with nature. It's a handsome edition."

Bound in red leather with gold lettering, it bore an inscription on the flyleaf in her grandfather's handwriting.

When you have finished wandering, Paul, these may carry a message for you. In friendship,
Martin.

Sarah was touched and thanked him with shining eyes.

"I shall treasure it. I remember my grandfather reciting one of Davies's poems to me once. A funny little ditty. It was called 'School's Out.' He was a marvelous speaker of verse. I owe it to him, my introduction to the rewards of poetry."

"Yes. It was odd that he, so rooted in his home and this county, should become a wanderer, too, after his wife died. I don't think he could bear any reminders. Theirs was a rare partnership."

He fell silent, and Sarah, thinking how gray his face looked, said gently, "Are you finding this party too tiring?"

"A little confusing, perhaps. I've spent so many years away from what we call civilization that I'm a bit at sea. Too old to adjust now, I'm afraid. Better for the children, perhaps, to have brought their friends so that they can enjoy themselves in their own way. I'd hoped ... But never mind. They're strangers to me, you know, except for Simon. Can't expect anything else."

"The generation gap is always difficult to bridge."

"But not with you, Sarah. That's odd, isn't it?"

"Perhaps because you see my grandfather in me."

"The generation gap. Was there one between you and your parents?"

"A chasm, I'm afraid. They weren't happy together, my parents. They quarrelled terribly. It used to frighten me. I escaped into a land of make-believe. Spun stories and had imaginary friends. Except at holiday times when I came down here and had real ones. The Rannocks. And a real home with my grandparents."

He nodded, leaning on his stick, then looked up at the sound of footsteps on the path.

"Goodness, here comes Jove, looking like a thunder cloud," said Sarah as Simon loomed up in the dusk.

"You all right, Dad?" he said, his eyes searching his father's face.

"Quite all right, thanks. Just having a breath of air with Sarah. It's getting dark and clammy, though. I'll get back now."

Simon walked back to the house with them, then laid a detaining hand on Sarah's shoulder.

"Come for a walk with me, Sarah. I need some exercise."

It was more of a peremptory order than a request, but she accompanied him down the drive and out into the lane.

"What sort of shoes have you got on?" he asked abruptly.

"Reasonable for walking, but not suitable for muddy fields or climbing the downs."

"Let's walk as far as the bridge, then. I need your calming presence."

"I hope it's safe to walk with you. I feel you may explode at any moment. And I must warn you that I'm feeling very fragile. That wine has had a treacherous aftermath as far as I'm concerned. I have to put my feet down gently."

They walked along the lane in silence, leaving the lights of the hamlet behind them. A gentle breeze stirred the bare branches above their heads, weaving a pattern across the stars and the crescent moon. A short distance down the lane, a side path led them on to a humped bridge across the river. There they stopped, leaning on the wooden balustrade. A little clucking sound from a moorhen broke the silence. Across the dark water gliding beneath them, the moon cast a shimmering path. With the cool touch of the night air on her face and the sweet half-rotting river smell about her, Sarah went into a dreamy trance until Simon shattered it.

"And what do you think of this happy family reunion, Sarah?"

She reflected, choosing her words carefully.

"The bits of the jigsaw don't really fit together very well, do they?"

"Brian and Katie never intended that they should. But perhaps they're the realists. There's safety in numbers. I'm sorry for the old man. Not what he intended at all. And even as a party, this one wouldn't jell in a month of Sundays. Donald and Alison have retired with Debbie and the Christmas tree to Dad's study while the theatrical party is putting on a musical act of deafening volume in the sitting room, and Brian and his young woman are practicing putting in the hall. A very odd miscellany indeed, for which we are indebted mainly to my young sister. Katie," he added grimly, "should have been spanked more when she was young."

"Wouldn't have made any difference. There's a something in Katie that is not tamable and never was."

"Maybe. When I get her alone, though, I'm going to have a good try at sorting her out. So far, I haven't been able to corner her."

"I'm not surprised, with that look in your eyes. She evidently thought she was doing you a favor."

"Without any previous word to any of us. For cool nerve, Katie takes the biscuit. And you stand aside, watching our antics with thoughtful eyes. What do you think of your cherished Rannock family now?"

"An interesting lot," said Sarah calmly. "I'd like to know them better, but I don't find them completely divorced from the children I knew. Brian is the only one I don't feel I know any more. There are enough recognizable bits in the rest of you to make me feel at home."

"And when you've had enough of them, you can always escape to nature," he said, gently mocking, his mood softening now.

"Yes. Look, Simon. Isn't that beautiful?"

She touched his arm as three white swans glided from beneath the bridge and proceeded upstream, pale and ghostly in the moonlight. Simon said nothing but put an arm around her shoulders as they watched until the swans disappeared around a bend in the river.

"How mild it is! Like spring. A green Christmas. Need some hard frost to break up the ground, Jeff Murcia says, but I like this gentle weather," said Sarah.

They walked back up the lane arm in arm, at peace together. Just before reaching the entrance to Marlyn Manor, Simon turned her to face him and kissed her gently.

"Thank you, Sarah."

"What for?"

"You wouldn't understand if I told you. Shall we say, a touch of balm? I feel better for it."

In the drive, they met Anna Pirano.

"Your father said he thought you'd gone out for a walk, Simon. It seemed a good idea to see if I could find you. Haven't had a chance to talk to you all day."

"Such a crowd," said Simon politely.

"It's a lovely night. Do come a little way with me."

"Of course. Come along, Sarah. I like a woman on each arm."

"I really ought . . ." she began.

"Nonsense," said Simon firmly, taking her arm in a tight grip. "You've shouldered enough chores today. Let's walk as far as the church. That will be far enough in those high heels of yours, Anna."

Sarah could almost feel the waves of anger from Anna as they retraced their steps along the lane.

"It's so good to see you again, Simon," she said. "You don't know how much I've been looking forward to this Christmas ever since Katie invited me."

"And when was that?" asked Simon politely.

"Only a week ago. I'd just arrived here, and we decided to keep it secret."

"Are you staying in England long?"

"That depends."

"Is your husband in England, too?"

"That's what I came . . . Hasn't Katie told you . . ."

She seemed confused, and Sarah wished that Simon had not enforced her presence, for Anna was making it increasingly clear that she had intimate matters to discuss with Simon and that Sarah was an embarrassing outsider.

"Hasn't Katie told me what?"

"That Carlo died of a heart attack two months ago."

There was a pause. Simon's steps did not slacken and his arm held Sarah's as tightly as ever. His voice was still the polite voice of an acquaintance. Whatever he might be feeling, his control was superb.

"My condolences. A terrible shock for you. Or was his health more precarious than his age and appearance suggested?"

"It was the second attack in six months."

"I'm so sorry. At forty-five, with his wealth and position and you, Anna, he had so much to live for. No children?"

"No."

"A lot of responsibility for you, his estate and business affairs, but I expect you have good support from his family."

"I'd like to talk to you about it some time, Simon. Ask your advice."

"I'm afraid I'm in no position to advise you about

your late husband's affairs. I'm sure you have expert advisers."

Sarah could feel the tension in the air like an electric current although Simon changed the subject and drew her into the conversation by asking about the progress of her book and telling Anna about it. The response of the latter was brief and of a chilling politeness, and it was with relief that Sarah escaped when they returned to the house. Finding Debbie wandering around looking rather lost, a new teddy bear clasped tightly to her, Sarah found a quiet corner by the diningroom fire and told her a story about the children in the book she was writing. She proved a responsive listener, and Sarah found the absorbed expression of that small face a reassuring omen for the appeal of her characters. They were both enjoying themselves so much that when Alison tracked them down, even the prospect of helping her father cut the Christmas cake met with a lukewarm response from Debbie and some reluctance in Sarah to leave her imaginary world.

While they had tea, Sarah sat back in her favorite role of observer and reviewed this gathering of Rannocks and friends. How attractive Katie was with her vivacity and her pretty laughing voice. Beside her, Max Raigarth was viewing Anna over his cup of tea with an assessing eye. Sarah was not sure that she took to Max. He was a tall, striking-looking man, with black hair framing a square, powerful face. His mouth, she thought, suggested a cruel element, and his eyes watched Anna with a cool sensuality.

Anna would draw men's eyes wherever she went. Tall enough to offset the generous curves of her figure, the smooth black hair was swept up to emphasize the perfect oval of her face, with its bold features and olive complexion. Her lustrous dark brown eyes were heavy-lidded, and her lips had generous inviting curves. A passionate, smouldering beauty was there. That she could create havoc in a man's life was not surprising. And that, whatever their past history, she was now bent on picking up the threads again with Simon was quite evident.

Sarah's eyes moved to Simon, who was on the other side of the room talking to Brian and Joan. His taut leanness made Brian look fleshy and blurred beside him. She liked his clear-cut hawkish looks. Crisp and stripped for action. And if she was wary of his harsh moods and sometimes angered by his domineering ones, she realized that harsh circumstances and heavy responsibilities had molded his armor and often experienced an aching longing to penetrate that armor and bring to his eyes more often the softness which she sometimes evoked.

Simon and Anna. Would Anna bring happiness back into his life? The thought brought a warning stab. She saw him look away from Joan and followed the direction of his gaze. Anna was looking at him, a small secret smile on her lips. Simon's face was hard to read. His mouth looked grim, and it might have been the light from the lamp beside him that put that gleam in his eyes. Sarah shivered, feeling out of her depth.

"You've cast a spell over Debbie with your story," said Alison, coming to sit beside her. "She can't stop talking about the children who live in the corner house of The Avenue."

After some hilarious charades that evening, they played records and danced in the hall, the theatrical members having brought a record player and suitable music.

"Been a very jolly day, after all," said Brian, dancing with Sarah toward the end of the evening.

"Yes."

"Managed to cheer up this dismal old place. It's never been as lively as this in its history before. We're actually hearing music and laughter! I wonder the walls haven't caved in from shock."

"It wasn't as bad as that, surely."

"Worse than you could imagine, Sarah. Poor old Ma. I suppose she couldn't help it. Had a pretty rough deal. How we enjoyed escaping to Rylands, though."

"And now? A brighter landscape, I imagine."

"True. Know what I vowed when I left home, Sarah? To find a cheerful job. Didn't care what it was as long as I was surrounded with lively characters and could indulge in simple pleasures."

"Such as?"

"Sport. Golf, as it's turned out. A friendly bar. Cheerful mates. Believe me, this house cured me of any desire for earnest endeavor. I like life easy and pleasant and don't probe deeper than that. Life's a comedy, Sarah. Doesn't do to lose sight of that."

His face was flushed and drink had given him an air of jovial abandon.

"Funny ha-ha or peculiar?"

"Both. Just don't take it seriously. That's my creed. Skim the cream off if you can but never delve down. You're pretty, Sarah. Gold lights in your eyes and your hair. My childhood sweetheart."

"I don't remember that. I seem to remember a few fights."

"Always liked you. Come under the mistletoe and let me kiss you to make up for the fights."

He kissed her with more expertise than she had expected, then drew her closer as they went on dancing until Joan tapped him on the shoulder and said, smiling, "Time for a switch. It's ladies' choice this time."

Donald, just abandoned, dutifully teamed up with Sarah and steered her with uninspired efficiency round the hall. Over his shoulder, she saw Anna dancing with Simon, molded to him as though made of plasticine. Nobody claimed Donald, and Sarah danced with him to the end of the record, after which Katie and Max entertained them with a burlesque of a twenties' tango, performed with deadly serious, passionate abandon, Max looking every inch a Rudolph Valentino and Katie, with a willowy grace, conveying a mixture of fear and adoration. It was superbly done, and even Paul Rannock, who looked deathly tired, was moved to laughter.

"What a lively spirit my youngest has!" he said to Sarah.

"Yes. She was certainly born under a dancing star."

"Well, it's good to see the young people enjoying themselves so wholeheartedly."

"You look very tired."

"Yes, I am. I'll slip away, I think. Nobody will miss me. Goodnight, my dear. Go and enjoy yourself with the young folk."

He patted her shoulder affectionately and made his way round the hall, pausing for a few words with Alison before he went slowly up the stairs.

The party broke up soon after midnight, and Simon walked to Rylands with Katie and Sarah.

"How sweet and old-fashioned of you, Simon," said Katie wickedly. "I can't think hidden dangers lurk for Sarah and me in this peaceful little hamlet."

"You are more than capable of dealing with anything that might turn up, my girl. I wanted a breath of fresh air before going to bed."

At some time during that evening, Sarah fancied, Simon had taken his young sister to task, for there was an air of defiance about her.

"A hangover?" she said sweetly. "I thought you seemed a little Scrooge-like this evening. Not really putting your heart into the festivities."

"If you're not careful, I'll dampen your festive spirit with a dip in the river," he said.

"What ingratitude after all my hard work on your behalf!" said Katie, the gate of Rylands now between her and Simon.

"Just remember one thing, Katie," said Simon, and he was not joking now. "Don't interfere in my affairs. Goodnight, Sarah."

"Well, well," said Katie blithely, as she followed Sarah up the path. "Caesar hath spoken." She gave a little yelp and clutched Sarah's arm. "Look at those eyes! Ghosts, or have I had too much to drink?"

"It's only Piper, my cat," said Sarah with amusement, as the glowing eyes moved from fence to ground level and Piper's furry body rubbed against her legs.

Sarah, ready for bed, found Katie as spritely as though the day had just dawned. She puttered around the cottage, exclaiming with delight and interest at various features, expressing approval of the spare room she was offered, then said, "It's all lovely and cozy and just like you, Sarah. And do you know, I can distinctly remember one or two things still, although I was such a babe when I was here. That grandfather clock, for instance. I remember I was fascinated by the shepherd and shepherdess dancing round the frame. And that picture over the fireplace of the moorland stream and the stag drinking. He looked so frightened, I used to think. And he still does."

"He's probably just heard the sound of the hunt. That's a painting of Exmoor, where my grandparents spent their honeymoon."

"It's all delightful and out of this world. Way back in the past, but sort of timeless. An Alice-in-Wonderland feeling. Although I only remember in snatches, I know we were happy here. Perhaps the only place where we were happy then. It was so different from our home. Shall we have a pot of tea before we go to bed and talk about old times?"

And so Sarah fetched a hotplate and placed it on the hearth and made a pot of tea. Katie, sitting on the hearthrug, recalled their childhood for a little, but she lived in the present too much to be drawn for long to the past and was soon chattering to Sarah about her stage career and her friends.

"Poor Sally and Jim. Wasn't it dreadful to be burgled? And they're such dears, both of them. Jim's a fine producer. He even manages to keep the peace, more or less, with Max, and that's some achievement I can tell you. Of course, Max is a marvelous actor so has to be humored."

"Do you get on well with him?"

"Max?" Katie considered, her head on one side. "When we're not scrapping, yes. We both share a love of the theater and he's helped me a lot as an actress. An attractive brute, wouldn't you say?"

"Yes, in a way. Powerful personality."

"M'm. He presents problems. Thinks he owns me. Sort of Henry Irving touch, mixed with Svengali."

"Sounds a dangerous mixture to me," said Sarah, laughing.

"That's what I like. A touch of danger. Adds spice to life. And isn't Simon livid with me over Anna? Talking of danger, I nearly lost my head today. Quite unreasonable, too. I was only thinking of him. He was madly in love with Anna, you know."

"Was he? Another cup?"

"Yes, please." Katie settled down with her second cup, her vivid face alight with eagerness to talk about her brother's love affair. "It was mutual, you know. The first time they met, it was wham! Straight in at the deep end. A real romance, and so unexpected for my brother, with his feet always so firmly on the ground, to fall in love at first sight. Mind you,

Anna's no ordinary person. Simon wasn't the only one swanning round her."

"And when was this?"

"Five years ago last October. I remember because I was eighteen, and they met at a little supper party Max gave for the cast after the first night of the play that gave me my very first professional part. Max played the lead. Mine was only a small part, of course, but Simon was there on the first night and came back stage afterward. Max invited him to join us, and Anna was there as a friend of Max. And they took one look at each other, and that was it. Fathoms deep in love," said Katie dramatically.

"I can't imagine Simon disclosing all this, but perhaps he was less reserved then."

"Not really. Anna confided in me. We became good friends. She found the stage glamorous and had time on her hands. Her father had been sent over here. Some appointment at the Italian Embassy. Anna had come with her parents but felt a bit at sea for a time. Hers is a family of some standing in Italy, and I think she missed the social life she'd been used to. Anyway, once Simon came on her scene, she didn't miss anybody."

"What went wrong?"

"Well, it was all very sad. For a year, I expected the news of their engagement weekly. Simon was pressing her, but she asked for more time. Then it came out. A marriage had been planned long since between Anna and an Italian count whose family had known Anna's family for years. You know the kind of setup. An old landed family, wealthy. A suitable alliance. Marriage with a struggling young English architect, of a different religion, simply was not in the cards as far as Anna's family was concerned."

"And Anna had kept this secret all the time?"

"Yes. Oh, she was wretched about it, but she was so much in love and she wanted to have that year, at least."

"Poor Simon. I doubt whether he appreciated her reasoning."

"He spent the next year trying to dissuade her from the arranged match and wore himself and her ragged. But she couldn't go against her family, and tradition, and couldn't contemplate living in England, divorced from her own culture and Catholic religion, living in a modest way. I could understand her decision, but Simon couldn't. She came to me one day, looking as deathly as Juliet on her tomb, and broke down completely. They'd had a final, devastating row; she had refused to change her decision, and that was the end. I don't think Simon ought to have been so savage. Men are so conceited. They think the gift of themselves outweighs everything. Anna's marriage with her Italian count brought her wealth and status and a lovely estate in the country of her birth and religion.

"And all the pressure of her family was behind it. Still, it was sad, and Simon's had a rough deal all his life, really. That was why I was delighted when Anna wrote to me. At least I wasn't delighted that her husband had died, that would be too heartless, but I was delighted that it gave Simon another chance. Anna still feels the same about him. I thought he'd be overjoyed to see her again and learn that she's free."

"Three years is long enough for feelings to change."

"Yes, but his haven't, I'm sure. It's just wounded pride at having been turned down once. As I said, men are so vain. He'll come round, though. And won't it be delightful to have a sister-in-law with a gorgeous estate in Italy? Not far from the coast in beautiful country. The gardens are a dream, Anna says. Fountains and shady walks and terraces and exotic flowers. I visualize blissful holidays when I'm resting between parts."

"You're jumping ahead a bit, aren't you?"

"Oh, Simon will come out of his injured pride soon enough. Anna will see to that. A lovely wife who loves him as passionately as he loves her, a fine estate in a delectable country, and never any financial worries for the rest of his life. What more could a man ask? And Simon deserves it."

"He might not want to leave England and his work here."

"Not want to escape from this awful climate to a lovely estate in Italy? After all, architects can work anywhere, but I should have thought looking after the estate and Anna's affairs would give him all the occupation he needed. Anna will soon heal that injured pride. She knows how to handle men, and she's very, very sexy, don't you think?"

"Yes. Well, I'm for bed," she said firmly, for Katie appeared to be set for what remained of the night, and Sarah was aware of feeling very tired. It seemed a long time since she had set out that morning for Marlyn Manor to help Alison with the Christmas dinner. So many new faces, so much to take in about the members of the family who had played such an important part in her childhood, learning what the years between had brought about.

In spite of her tiredness, her mind did not want to shut off in bed that night. All the new impressions kept moving through her thoughts, and foremost was the history of Simon and Anna Pirano. But her last thoughts before she finally fell asleep were of her grandparents and this cottage, which had played such a happy part in their lives. All of them, Alison, Katie, Brian, Simon, in their different ways had remembered those days with affection, like a distant song which could still warm their hearts as it warmed hers.

Her grandparents had been kind, loving people. They had loved each other dearly, as the journals revealed if memory had needed any further confirmation, and their love had spread out to warm them all. She would like to think that they knew how much they had meant to five children whose homes had been unhappy, knew that their distant song was still remembered and for her would always echo around this cottage, which was now her home.

CHAPTER EIGHT

SARAH DISCOVERED THAT if Katie seemed tireless at night, in the morning it was a different matter, and it was mid-morning before she tumbled down to breakfast. She revived quickly after coffee and toast, which was all she ever had for breakfast, she declared, and they set off for Marlyn Manor, cheered by a pale wintry sunshine which polished the ivy swarming up the trees in the lane and brought a glitter to the river. Soon, thought Sarah, the first celandines would be appearing at the foot of the hedgerow.

On the way, they caught a glimpse of Anna and Simon, walking together along the far bank of the river.

"There," said Katie blithely. "What did I say?"

"A whole lot. That looks like the rest of your party behind."

By the bridge, Max caught sight of Katie and hailed her.

"Hi, Katie! Come and help me bear all this fresh air."

"Coming?" asked Katie of Sarah.

"You go. I want to give Alison these lettuces before lunch."

"Did you grow them?"

"Jeff Murcia did, in the greenhouse."

"Come on, Katie," called Max imperiously.

Katie flashed a smile at Sarah and ran off to join him.

At Marlyn Manor, Alison was on her own, busily

putting the house to rights after the chaos of the previous night.

"Brian and Joan went off early to have a round of golf somewhere. Father and Don are in the garden with Debbie. Don's fixed up a swing for her. What a mess," she added, gathering up a pile of assorted refuse used in the charades the previous night. "Katie's friends just seem to leave everything where it drops."

"Shall I see to the salad?" asked Sarah.

"Thanks, dear. We shall have a bit of peace this evening, anyway. They're all leaving after an early cup of tea. They've arranged to go to a show in London."

"Your father will be disappointed."

"I don't think so. He's come down to earth. There's something sticky on the carpet here. And look at the burn marks on this table. That man Max must have stubbed out his cigarettes on it."

"Never mind. It will give Mrs. Pilsen something to moan over when she gets back."

Alison pushed back a strand of hair from her forehead and smiled bleakly.

"Sorry if I'm a bit crotchety. Brian annoyed me this morning by cracking snide jokes about Don. He and Katie don't like him, you know. Don's worth a dozen of Brian any day of the week. He's loyal and dependable and always there, which is more than I can say for my family, Simon excepted. With a father who showed me what marriage was like when the husband was never there, I married for security and a kind, caring home for my children. I get fed up with this sharpshooting at Don. He's a splendid husband. I couldn't wish for a better," said Alison defiantly.

She must have been deeply hurt by Brian's jokes at her husband's expense to lose her customary composure, and Sarah put an arm round her shoulders.

"You don't have to worry. You're the fortunate one. Your world is stable. I get the impression that Katie and Brian have no stable center."

Alison smiled her gratitude.

"You're right. I shouldn't blame them. Their upbringing and home life didn't help them to think of anybody but themselves. For my children, it shall be different."

"How many do you aim to have?" asked Sarah, smiling.

"Three. And I think I've started the second now, but don't say anything until I'm sure."

As lunchtime approached, Sarah went into the garden to find Paul Rannock and see how he had weathered the Christmas Day party. It was very quiet out there on that calm morning, and as she walked along by the thick overgrown hedge which fronted the lane, Anna's voice reached her clearly in urgent tones.

"Wait a minute before we go in, Simon. It's so difficult to be alone with you here and I must talk to you."

"We said all that had to be said three years ago, Anna."

"But everything's changed now. We belong to each other, darling. We always did. Now there's nothing to keep us apart except your pride, and surely you're not going to let that override our need for each other. I'm ready to take a certain amount of blame, although you'll never understand how difficult my position was. Things are different in your country. But now that it's all come miraculously right, why are you behaving like this?"

"Now that you can have your cake and eat it, you mean?"

"Share it with you, my love. That's all I ever wanted in my heart."

"You can't throw something away and then expect to find it the same when you retrieve it."

"It needn't have been a complete break. I told you. With discretion . . ."

"Having an affair with a married woman is not my way. What do you take me for, Anna? To think I'd be a party to that sort of deception, contented with a bone thrown now and again when your husband wasn't looking."

"I know, darling. But can't you please forget the past and enjoy what is within our reach now?"

"Time brings change, Anna. What you did changed me. You can't rewrite history."

"Then," said Anna caressingly, "let's start a new era. I know you still love me. It's in your eyes when you look at me. Kiss me, Simon."

And at that stage, Sarah moved quickly and quietly away, ashamed at having lingered, realizing how deeply she was now involved with Simon to have been unable to move out of earshot sooner.

At the end of the garden, she found Donald pushing Debbie on a swing he had rigged up on an overhanging branch of an oak tree. Paul Rannock was sitting on the seat nearby. He smiled when he saw her and assured her that he felt fine although he looked drawn.

"A lovely soft morning," she said, sitting down beside him.

"It is, indeed. When I was in the tropics at Christmas, I always envisaged the English countryside white with frost or blanketed with snow at this time of the year. It was a nice cooling thought. But, of course, seldom borne out by the facts. My picture of it was Dickensian. I was completely out of touch. I hope you're enjoying your Christmas here, my dear."

"Very much. A jolly party, and it's been good to see Brian and Alison and Katie again."

"Yes, I think they're enjoying themselves. I haven't had a chance to talk to them much, but they all seem to have found their feet in the world and to be happy enough."

His eyes looked sad, but she felt that he had now calmly accepted the fact that although his children might have needed him in the past when he wasn't there, they did not need him now. And she knew he would be blaming nobody but himself for that. He smiled now as Debbie ran up to show him an acorn she had just picked up. He explained how squirrels liked to bury them for winter food, told her that it would grow into a tree like the one she had been swinging on if she planted it, and watched while she carefully scooped out a hole among rotting leaves and buried it. She took his hand as they all walked back toward the house, listening intently while he told her about the trees in the jungle and the wild animals that roamed there. Sarah was glad that the little girl had overcome her fear of him and bridged the gap that Brian and Katie were not able to bridge.

With the visitors making preparations to go that afternoon, Sarah found herself alone with Katie in the kitchen when they were joined by Anna.

"Any luck, Anna? Have you persuaded Simon to come with us?" asked Katie.

"No. He feels he must see Christmas out with his father, as promised."

"He's so stubborn," sighed Katie. "But I must confess I'm amazed at his reactions. It's all right," she added as Anna shot a glance at Sarah. "Sarah's like a sister. One of the family from way back. I hope Simon's not going to stay in this mood for long."

"He won't," said Anna with a confident little smile.

"Sure?" asked Katie.

"Quite sure. Max has lost his car keys. Any idea where they might be?"

"Yes. On the chest in the hall. I took them out of his pocket to open up the trunk."

Anna left them and Katie continued to clean up the shoes, which had suffered from the morning's walk along the river bank. It was a good thing, Sarah thought, that Alison was not there to see twigs, leaves, and mud missing the newspaper, which Katie had spread on the table, only to fall on the floor as Katie brandished her shoe while she talked.

"Won't it be exciting to have a really grand wedding in the family? A fairytale scenario. The bride, a beautiful Contessa with what sounds like a palace for a home and untold wealth."

"You're very positive about it," said Sarah, thinking that twenty-three years had put no brake on Katie's vivid imagination.

"Oh, there's no doubt that he'll marry her. The only question is how long he'll play the injured party. Not long, judging by the gleam of triumph in Anna's eyes just now. I never thought he'd be anything but overjoyed, but I suppose it came as a bolt out of the blue, and he couldn't really take it in and forget their last meeting."

"He might not feel the same now as he did three or four years ago."

"That could be the case with a good many people. I mean, I fall in and out of love regularly. But Simon's not like that. He doesn't commit himself easily, but when he does, it goes deep and is for keeps. And believe me, it went deep with Anna. Besides, look what strong cards she has. Given the feeling between them, what sane man would resist?"

"I'm not an authority on such matters. I lead a very simple life," said Sarah with a little twinkle, which drew Katie's eyes sharply to her.

"You're getting at me," she declared.

"Never," said Sarah, laughing. "I enjoy the fruits of your dramatic experience of the world."

"All right. All right," said Katie, with a flashing smile. "But life needs a little dramatizing if it's not to be drab, and I really am thrilled at the prospect of having anybody as exciting and glamorous as Anna in the family."

It seemed to be something of an anti-climax, after Katie and Brian and their friends departed. They played Scrabble, looked at a television program, listened to some music. Sarah, watching Simon, tried to gauge his feelings, but he gave nothing away. He might be overjoyed at Anna's reappearance in his life or he might be angry, but there was nothing to be deduced from his reserved demeanor that evening. Wondering what had happened on the other side of the hedge after she had withdrawn that morning, she was conscious of a heartache. She could discount much of Katie's over-dramatization of the circumstances, but it seemed to her all too likely that Anna would win him back again. Perhaps already had, for she had looked very confident that afternoon.

He got up automatically to walk home with her that night although his preoccupied manner made her say that it was not necessary. His attitude seemed to indicate that she was now accepted as a young relation of the family, and it was his duty to see her safely home as though she were still a child, to be safely returned from a children's party. He brushed aside her efforts to excuse him from this duty, and they walked out into a dark night with a hint of rain in the air.

"Well, it didn't go off so badly, after all," she said, bottling down an annoyance which she knew was unreasonable.

"No. Not quite what my father expected, but

perhaps it was as well to have a crowd."

"A bright and breezy lot, anyway, Katie's friends."

"Yes. Theatrical people live in a world of their own."

"Katie's still a child, though."

"And a crazily irresponsible one."

"She means well."

"Don't mouth platitudes, Sarah. I don't expect them from you."

"I thought I was merely speaking the truth."

"Then you're more obtuse than I thought. She's as mischievous as a monkey, that one, and you, who knew her as a child and have seen her again now, must know it."

"I wouldn't say mischievous. She sees life as a drama. Doesn't seem to know where drama ends and reality begins. She loves to dramatize."

"That's better. But the effect can be mischievous because she doesn't limit her dramatizing to her own life. What did you think of Brian?"

Since platitudes were evidently not the order of the day, she thought carefully, then said, "His boat has a shallow draft, but he'll see that it stays afloat in calm and pleasant waters, I guess."

"You're right there. The old man took the invasion very well, I thought."

"Yes. It answered some questions for him, and brought him some consolation in the form of his granddaughter. He and Debbie have got on very happily together today. I'm glad about that. Alison says she'll bring Debbie over more often in future."

"That's good. Must say I hadn't noticed."

He was too preoccupied with Anna to notice much that Christmas, she thought. It was beginning to drizzle, and he didn't linger when they reached Rylands.

"Goodnight, Sarah. Thanks again for your help."

Deposited safely and in good order, she thought, as he strode off before she could say anything more. She walked up the path feeling chilled and unhappy. Anna's confidence, she thought, was well-founded.

CHAPTER NINE

ON NEW YEAR'S DAY, Sarah had an unexpected visitor. She was working on her book in the afternoon when a knock at the door revealed Nick Barbury. She smiled delightedly.

"On my way home after a New Year's Eve party at my cousin's last night, so thought I'd look in to wish you a happy New Year and inquire after the book."

Settled in an armchair by the fire, he looked around him with approval, noting the papers on the table in the window.

"Am I interrupting your work?"

"I was only correcting yesterday's stint. I usually work in a little room at the back, but it was so cold today that I brought it in here."

"All very nice and snug. Had a job to find the cottage until a chap at the pub enlightened me. Went through this place once without noticing it and found myself in the next village. It's a peaceful retreat. Happy here?"

"Very. I feel as though I've picked up the threads where my grandparents left off."

"And how's the book coming on?"

"I'm pleased with it. At least, as pleased as one ever is with one's own work. It's come alive, anyway. And Paul Rannock, I've discovered, is a fine artist and is doing some irresistible drawings for it. I sent one up to my publisher, Mr. Birch, a few days ago and he telephoned me yesterday to give me his enthusiastic approval."

"Splendid. But what about Rannock's book?"

"Making slow progress. To tell you the truth, he seems more interested in illustrating mine than in writing his. He found my grandfather's journal fascinating. Took him right back to his youth, and that's where he seems to enjoy being these days."

"Well, I'm sure you're capable of steering his book along as well as your own."

"I didn't know you had any relations in this part of the world."

"My cousin, Alison. She and her husband live at Foulding, a few miles the other side of Dilford."

"I know it. A pretty village."

"Her husband, Silas Helmsdale, is a landscape architect with a practice in Dilford, and I discovered quite by chance that a chap named Rannock had recently joined the partnership. One of your Rannocks?"

"Yes. Simon. It's a small world."

"Silas thinks well of him."

"Do you see much of your cousin?"

"She doesn't often get me down here, but my grandmother in Surrey holds monthly tea parties for the clan, at which we are all expected to be present unless we have a very good excuse, so we keep in touch."

"You surprise me. I've always thought of you as a lone wolf. Never imagined you were one of a large family and certainly not the type to keep close ties with relatives."

"Our matriarch gives us no option. Anyway, I'm rather fond of the clan, or most members of it. In small doses, of course. Its tentacles stretch from Surrey to Northumberland, but Grandma manages to bind them at the center. A formidable old lady. Maintains the standards of earlier times and yields nothing to the more permissive ways of today. When she goes, it may fall apart, but I hope not."

They were easy with each other, the embarrassment of their last encounter a thing of the past. She no longer ached for what he could not give but welcomed him as an old friend with whom she could discuss her work, fond of him but able to say goodbye until the next time without a pang. She realized this with certainty and a faint surprise. She had moved on. And Nick, with his sensitive antennae, had realized it, too, she thought as his eyes met hers and his words carried a warm sincerity. There would be no awkwardness between them again. Only a strand of friendship that might be tenuous but which she hoped would never break.

"Would you care to look through the first chapters of my book while I get some tea?" she asked. "I'd like your opinion."

"Sure."

He settled down with the pages of typescript while she went out to the kitchen to prepare tea. When she returned with a cart laden with buttered toast, tea, and a fruitcake, he was absorbed and went on reading through his first cup of tea, refusing food for the moment. She watched him anxiously, knowing that from Nick she would get nothing but his honest opinion where writing was concerned, and he was a stern critic.

"Congratulations, Sarah," he said, putting it aside and helping himself to a piece of toast. "Well written, delightfully real characters, and a feeling for the period which will make it a winner with parents as well as children, I guess, in view of the present mood of nostalgia. A great advance on your first. Your grandfather's journal has evidently inspired you."

"Yes. I'm loving every minute of it."

"That comes through. I'm glad you've disciplined your weakness for adjectives, though I notice you're still having to watch it, judging from the crossings out."

"I know. Over-enthusiasm for the subject makes me elaborate too much."

"Try to retain a certain detachment. Economy of style, with every word telling. That's what we have to aim at. That stimulates the reader's imagination whereas over-elaboration with a bombardment of adjectives and adverbs merely flattens it."

"Poets show us the way, but how difficult it is!"

"That's what makes it so fascinating. The challenge."

"Anyway, I'm absolutely delighted that you give me a good grade for this effort."

"An A-minus at the very least."

"Praise indeed!"

They were interrupted by a knock at the door. It was Simon. She had hoped he might come, knowing that he was at Marlyn Manor that day, and welcomed him with a smile.

"Am I intruding?" he asked, glancing at Nick's coat on the hall chest. "You've a visitor?"

"An old friend, Nick Barbury. Come and meet him. He's related to the wife of your senior partner, Helmsdale."

Introductions accomplished, Simon glanced at the scattered typescript and said, "I'm interrupting you. I won't stay. Just wanted to wish you a happy New Year, Sarah."

"Thank you. And I wish you the same. But you're not interrupting, and you must stay to tea. Nick was just giving me his professional opinion of my book, which I am glad to say is favorable."

"Pontificating about writing, she means, which is a very foolish thing to do," drawled Nick, leaning back at his ease and eyeing Simon with the calm air of detachment so familiar to Sarah.

She wondered what Simon would think of this fair-haired aesthete who dressed with such uncommon elegance. At first sight, he easily could be taken for a rather affected literary dilettante, but nothing was farther from the truth. Would Simon sense the shrewd intelligence and single-mindedness which lay behind the urbane exterior? She watched the two of them with some amusement as they discussed architecture over their buttered toast. Simon's dark, alert hawkishness contrasted so strongly with Nick's handsome, indolent air that the juxtaposition of the two men intrigued her. It was like watching a reclining, decorative Russian wolfhound and an alert, wary Alsatian coming to terms with each other.

Simon evidently still seemed to harbor the feeling that he was intruding, however, for he left within the hour although she guessed he had originally come over for the evening.

"Quite impressive, the eldest Rannock," observed Nick, when she returned from seeing Simon off.

"Yes. We're good friends."

Nick eyed her speculatively, but said no more about Simon, turning the conversation to Paul Rannock and his memoirs. Sarah, now cut off from literary circles, enjoyed the opportunity of talking shop, and time slipped by so quickly that Nick's dropping-in extended until half-past ten, and then he had difficulty getting his car to start.

"It's been giving me trouble this past week. Some electrical fault, I think," he said, investigating the engine of the red M.G. while Sarah hovered sympathetically nearby. "Don't stay out here and catch cold, my dear."

"I'll go and brew up some coffee to sustain you," she said.

It took him the best part of an hour to find the trouble and get the car to start.

"Hope it'll see you home," she said.

"Not to worry. It's been good to find you so well and happy, Sarah. When you've made your name with that book, I shall be able to bask in your reflected glory and claim you for my protégée."

"I shall be quite contented if my publishers like it and it provides me with enough income to be able to write the next one. I don't go much for glory. I like a quiet, simple life."

"I can see you do. You're very wise."

Unexpectedly, he bestowed a light kiss on her cheek before sliding into the driving seat.

"If you're down this way, Nick, there's always a warm welcome for you at Rylands. Always."

"Bless you. I'll remember."

She watched the car lights disappear down the lane, and she lingered by the gate for a few minutes. It was a clear night, and myriads of stars glittered in the dark sky. The first day of the new year was ending. There were no sounds of revelry from the hamlet, no lights to be seen. Just a little murmuring breeze in the trees, and the canopy of stars above. Gladdened by Nick's visit, comforted by the realization that all pain had now gone out of that relationship, leaving only the warmth of friendship behind, she felt very much at peace with the world as she watched the constellations. She remembered some of the names still from her grandfather's teaching and recognized the extra brilliance of Sirius, dominating the sky. Whatever the new year brought, she thought, the past year had served her well in leading her to a home in this tranquil, beautiful place.

CHAPTER TEN

SARAH SAW NOTHING of Simon in the weeks that followed, although she learned from his father that he was at Marlyn Manor most weekends.

"He seems worried. Doesn't confide in me, but I have a nasty feeling that he's getting embroiled with that Italian girl again."

"What makes you think that?"

"Nothing tangible, but someone keeps phoning him every weekend here. I think it's Anna."

"Doesn't Simon say who it is?"

"Just a friend. That's all he says, in a tone that doesn't invite further inquiries. And I know he's been up to London several times these past weeks."

"You don't like the idea?"

"She created havoc in his life before."

"But circumstances are different now, according to what Katie told me."

"Maybe. I only want to see Simon happy. If marrying Anna Pirano would make him happy, that's fine. But he's not happy now. What worries me is the possibility that I'm an obstacle. Simon may feel that he can't go and live in Italy and leave me. I hope to goodness he doesn't think that. I can get along all right for what remains of my life although I should miss him greatly, of course. He hasn't discussed it with you, I suppose?"

"No. I haven't seen him for the past three or four weeks."

"Katie talked about it to you. What did she think?"

"That Simon would marry Anna, although his pride made his first reaction at Christmas an unpropitious one. Anna would bring him round, she said."

"She's a very attractive young woman. Well," he added, sighing, "we shall see. But if you get any hint that I'm a stumbling block, my dear, I trust you to let me know. I won't have any sacrifices for me."

"I think you're too prone to a sense of guilt. It makes you see yourself as a liability everywhere. Not true. I'm sure if Simon wants to marry Anna, he will do so."

"It's never easy for me to know what Simon is feeling, but I had fancied lately that he was growing fond of you, my dear."

"In a brotherly fashion."

"You and he have much more in common, I would say, than he and Anna Pirano."

"We're good friends. That's not quite the same, is it?"

"No. Would such an idea appeal to you?" he asked tentatively; then, as Sarah hesitated, he went on quickly, "No, I have no right to ask that. Forgive me. Wishful thinking on my part. It would make me so happy to see you and Simon marry. An old man's foolish dream, perhaps."

She was touched, as always, by his humility.

"I've become very fond of Simon," she said gently. "But I think his love is directed elsewhere. I could be wrong. I just don't know."

"Does that grieve you?"

She thought for a few moments, then said, "You have a seedling. With the right amount of sunshine and rain, you know it could grow into a beautiful plant. The knowledge of its potential is there."

"I understand perfectly. Thank you for your confidence, my dear. You know it will be respected."

"Of course. We understand each other. We always have."

"And that is a late bonus beyond all hope and expectation, for which I shall never cease to thank my stars."

She smiled and shook her head, and they returned to their work on the latest chapter of his memoirs. This they both agreed had fallen flat, and Sarah wanted to tighten it up, but although he agreed to all her amendments, she felt that his thoughts were elsewhere that morning. He was a fitful writer, she had discovered. Sometimes his old fervor for exploration would awaken, and he would write eagerly of his past discoveries; sometimes his interest seemed to flag and what he wrote was pedestrian and forced. She suspected, too, that since the Christmas reunion, he felt that his reason for writing this book seemed less valid. That his children now had established independent lives had been made plain to him, and he might well have concluded that the time for reparations was past.

It was not until a mild, sunny Saturday at the end of February that Sarah saw Simon again. She was planting a Japanese cherry tree in sight of the kitchen window when he strolled around the side of the cottage, and her heart leaped at the sight of him.

"Hello, stranger. I've missed you," she said, pausing in her efforts to drive in a stake.

His eyes lingered on her. In navy slacks and an old red sweater, muddy shoes, hair blown in the wind, mallet in hand, she hardly compared with the glamorous Anna, she thought. Suitably turned out for the kid sister role, though. Simon was looking well-tailored in a gray tweed suit. He usually dressed more casually at the weekend. Both his smile and his words, however, warmed her.

"I wonder what it is about you, Sarah, that is so refreshing. Allow me," he added, taking the mallet from her.

She smiled to herself as she watched him drive the stake home. Dear, managing Simon.

"If you'll hold the tree upright, I'll do the planting," she said firmly. "You're looking much too smart to do any grubbing."

"I've come straight from seeing a client this morning. Went over a site with him and then had lunch. What tree is this?"

"A flowering cherry tree, by name Oku Miyako, and it has pink buds and beautiful double white flowers and will gladden my eyes while I'm washing the dishes. And if I'm so refreshing, you don't seem to have been in need of refreshment lately."

"There are reasons."

Sarah spread out the roots of the tree carefully and shoveled compost out of the barrow into the prepared hole, firming it down as she went. When she had completed the task to her satisfaction, Simon fastened ties round the tree to the stake.

"Something very satisfying about planting a tree," said Sarah, standing back and surveying Oku Miyako with pleasure, already clothing it in her mind's eye with a mass of white blossom against a sunny blue sky.

"I agree."

"When I'm an old lady, I shall look at that tree, and give thanks."

"You still envisage being here then?"

"My roots are already deep down."

"On your own?"

"Who knows? I expect so. Scribbling my books, grubbing in the garden," she said lightly.

"You sound quite happy at the prospect. Has marriage no appeal?"

"I need notice of that question. Am I to have the pleasure of your company this afternoon or have you merely looked in?"

He looked at her with a quizzical expression as he

said, "I've a faint feeling of being in the doghouse. Why? Because I've neglected you?"

"Of course not. I know you're a busy person with other interests. I have no claim on your time," she said briskly, collecting up her tools and putting them in the wheelbarrow.

"Then I'm in the way. Spoiling your gardening."

"Don't be silly."

"Or perhaps you're expecting someone and I shall be one too many."

"Well, you know what a busy social life I lead here in this heavily populated area. And, of course, you can see that I'm dressed for the occasion."

He grinned and ruffled her hair.

"*Touché*. I wasn't being as fatuous as I sounded, though. After my visit a few weeks ago . . ."

"Eight weeks ago."

"As long as that?"

Their eyes met, each seeking an answer to unspoken questions. Then Sarah said gently, "I'll put these things away and clean up; then we'll have tea by the fire. It's getting chilly now the sun's going down."

It was not until his final cup of tea that Simon reverted to what was in both their thoughts.

"I haven't been round before, Sarah, because as well as having a civic-center job on my plate, which has taken me to Hampshire most Saturdays, I thought you were involved with Nick Barbury, that he was, after all, taking up his option, and I didn't want to barge in when not wanted. I'm right in supposing him to be the man in your life you once told me about?"

"Yes. But it seems to me that you were reading a lot into a chance visit from Nick."

"You looked so happy that evening."

"Because he'd read and praised my book, and I knew that his praise was never easily given and was worth having. And my writing means a lot to me."

"I see."

Something in his expression made her plunge into further explanations.

"It was quite by chance that he looked in. He was on his way back after a New Year celebration with the Helmsdales."

"Looked in? When I drove back to Dilford that night, his car was still here. It was late."

"And you thought?"

"That he'd gone beyond the point of being just a friend, and I'd better check up in future before casually dropping in. Silas Helmsdale speaks very highly of Nick, so I'll be happy if it's turning out as you wish, Sarah."

"What did you think of Nick?" she asked, thinking that few things were more discouraging than hearing the man you love express pleasure at the thought of your pairing off with another.

"Intelligent, witty, and excellent company. I wasn't sure that he might not be amusing himself with you, though. Not a man to reveal much of what goes on under that charming exterior, which was why I put out a few feelers in Silas's direction, and was totally reassured."

Sarah nearly choked over her tea at this brotherly concern, and her voice held a note of gentle irony not lost on him as she said, "I'm sorry you don't trust my judgment."

"Your judgment is usually very good indeed, but in my experience falling in love can act like dynamite on sound judgment."

"It's good of you to be so concerned," she said, feeling as though she were biting a very sour apple.

"Of course I'm concerned. I'm very fond of you. So is my father. I don't need to tell you, with your attachment to the Rannocks, that you're like one of the family."

"And so you feel responsible, as you always did?"

"You've said it. Don't get prickly. I can't help it. The pattern was established in our childhood."

"Ah, but I'm not any longer a child. But I'd hate you to get the picture wrong, Simon. Nick feels for me, as he always has, a detached friendship. My feelings have changed, though. Or perhaps not so much changed as seen for what they really are. I was half in love with Nick, but it was a very tenuous state. How could it be otherwise when he revealed so little of his inner self? That small candle went out for lack of oxygen. Once I'd come to grips with reality here at Rylands, it seemed like a pleasant little dream. I'm fond of Nick, he's helped me a lot in the past with my writing, and I enjoy talking literary shop with him. That's all. What lies underneath his delightful surface has never been revealed to me. Nick is, essentially, a loner. I'm happy with things as they are. A friendship based only on one common interest, writing, and one which we can take up at any time and enjoy without being bothered in the slightest by the long intervals between. Have I made myself clear?"

"Crystal clear. I jumped to the wrong conclusion. As bad as Katie. Must be a family failing. But you'll admit that there were reasonable grounds for my mistake in view of what you'd told me earlier."

"Yes. I'll keep you posted if there are any other contestants, just to see if you give them a pass certificate."

His eyes crinkled up in the way that always melted her as he laughed.

"Rebuke accepted. But nothing but the best is good enough for my girl, and however it riles you, I shall continue to be concerned. Which brings me to the other thing I wanted to talk to you about. I thought my father was looking more played out than usual last weekend. How has he been this week?"

"About the same as usual. Reluctant to start the

next chapter of his memoirs, though. He spent most of the week on another drawing for my book. A beauty. Ask him to show it to you. He's putting the finishing touches to it this weekend. I can't help wishing sometimes that he'd chosen to be an artist rather than an explorer. He has such talent. It's not only his craftsmanship, though that's superb, but his ability to evoke atmosphere. He brings to life so vividly the flavor of Edwardian childhood in these drawings."

"If he'd chosen to be an artist, our lives would have been very different, that's sure. How much of his memoirs remains to be written?"

"We're about two thirds of the way."

"Enough for a book?"

"Barely. And he has masses more material to be sorted out."

"I'll have another talk with him about it," said Simon abruptly. "Try to persuade him to cut it short."

"What's worrying you?"

"I'd sooner he didn't include his last expedition. It ended disastrously, he was nearly killed, and although it would make dramatic reading, to recall those experiences would put an appalling strain on him."

"You can dissuade him better than I."

"He's difficult, and stubborn. Reluctant to admit to what he sees as a weakness. Like knowing the ice on the lake is thin but driving himself to face the challenge, just to prove something. He knows my fears, so I suspect that with me he covers up. I can only rely on you to let me know if the cracks are appearing."

"Don't you think it's time you told me more so that I know more specifically what I'm looking for? After all, you've said that I'm as good as one of the family, and you know that what you tell me in confidence will go no farther."

"It's not a pretty story, but perhaps I should give you a few of the facts. I told you that on his last expedition to the tropics he fell into the hands of a remote, hostile tribe. I'm not going into any details, but he was tortured and unspeakable things were done to him. You've only seen his face. He was left for dead but was picked up by some friendly tribesmen, and eventually, by some miracle of endurance, got himself home. Once back, he collapsed and was ill for some time. But the shock was worse to his mind than his body. He had terrible nightmares. Would wake screaming. I had to live at Marlyn Manor during those early months. One night, when I went to him, he didn't know me and attacked me. For all his age and all that he'd suffered, he was still a strong man, and I was hard pressed when he suddenly realized who I was and collapsed, weeping.

"It had been touch and go whether I could keep him at home, but he hated hospitals or institutions of any kind and it seemed to me that he had a better chance of recovery in his own surroundings. After that alarming experience, though, he began to improve. He's not looked back, mentally I mean, and since you've come, he's been happier and more at peace than at any time since his return. For that, I'm deeply grateful to you, my dear. I don't think he'll have any relapse, but you can see why I would sooner those experiences were not revived. There's no good reason why they should be and plenty of reasons for leaving them buried."

"Thank you for telling me. I'll know what to look out for now."

"He's amazingly tough. The doctor thought he'd never survive that heart attack a year or so ago, but he came through. His state is precarious, though, and don't ever hesitate to phone me at the flat or the office if you're worried in any way. Mrs. Pilsen isn't all that I could wish as housekeeper, but it's not exactly an attractive job in that old barn of a house with a semi-invalid, and I doubt whether I could find anyone to take her place. That's why I'm so relieved to have you on the spot."

"In spite of trying to dissuade me at first, remember?"

"Very short-sighted of me. But I didn't know the old man would take you to his heart and I feared the strain of writing this book." He leaned forward to light a cigarette, then sank back into the armchair, his lean face showing signs of fatigue.

He had a lot on his mind, she thought. His work, his father, his affair with Anna Pirano, and, to her annoyance, a brotherly concern about her affairs. And if he took it upon himself to keep an eye on her, he divulged nothing of his own involvement with Anna. She would like to ask some questions for a change but could think of no tactful way of broaching the subject. She was searching her mind for words that would not seem crass or inquisitive when he picked up the book from the little table beside him.

"W. H. Davies. A favorite of yours?"

"Yes. Your father gave it to me for Christmas. It was originally a present from my grandfather to him."

"I well remember your grandfather's attempts to open our barbaric little minds to the rewards of poetry." He had opened the book at the marker, and now quoted,

"My walls outside must have some flowers,
My walls within must have some books;
A house that's small; a garden large,
And in it leafy nooks.
"Might have been written just for you."

"A not uncommon dream, I think. For me, it happens to have come true."

"And the reality hasn't proved disappointing."

"The reverse. Richly rewarding."

There was no mistaking the affection in his face as he rose, saying, "Wise Sarah, who not only knows what she wants but appreciates it when she's got it. Would we were all so blessed."

"I'd have said you knew what you wanted and moreover believed you knew what other people wanted, or ought to want, too."

He lifted his hands in laughing protest.

"A shocking indictment. I'll ignore that little jab and confess that I've been badly off course in the past, which should have taught me not to be so cocksure."

"But often blown off it by circumstances not of your making, I'm sure. You've had so many demands made of you."

"A few kind words for me, after all."

His eyes teased her and she shook her head.

"We don't need flattery between us."

"Quite right. You always do me good, Sarah. Do you know that? There's something very reassuring in the air at Rylands. Always was, for that matter. You carry on the tradition. I'd rather stay for the evening, but I must get back to the old man. He wants to discuss some business matters with me this evening."

She walked out to the car with him. It was nearly dark, with a dull red stain low down in the western sky. Blackbirds were making their last defiant calls before going to roost. The cluster of snowdrops by the gate gleamed palely against some ivy leaves. Simon lingered for a moment, studying the sky, and she was filled with a sudden aching for him that left her shaken. She wanted to keep him with her, to feel his arms around her, to bask in the warmth of his presence. But in a few moments she was watching the car disappear down the lane, and then all was silence around her.

In front of the fire, with Piper on her lap for

comfort, she reflected that she had learned nothing of his involvement with Anna, but it had been made absolutely plain that his involvement with *her* was of a brotherly nature only. She would have to be content with his friendship, which was warm and staunch enough and which she valued, but her own feelings went far beyond that. If she had not realized its full extent before, she now faced the truth that she loved Simon Rannock, deeply and irretrievably and hopelessly as far as its fulfillment was concerned. Protective and affectionate, he would be. And exasperating and teasing, too. But he would always see her as the childhood friend of the family and keep an eye on her as he might keep an eye on Katie. The vital element was lacking, and she was too realistic to hope that it would ever be any different.

Piper lifted up his head in ecstasy as she stroked the fur under his chin with a gentle finger. When she stopped, he stood up and paddled his paws on her thighs, not always sheathing his claws, until he found a comfortable position and settled down again with a steady purr to gaze into the fire. She could feel the vibrating warmth of his body through her slacks as she, too, gazed into the flames seeing what might have been, trying to reconcile herself to so much less.

CHAPTER ELEVEN

IN THE FIRST week of March, as though to spite the signs of spring in gardens and hedgerows, the weather veered from the mild pattern of the winter months, the wind blew from the north, the temperature plunged, and the snow came. Four inches fell in two days, settling on the branches, weighing down the shrubs, obliterating the almond blossom and all but the sturdiest of the budding daffodils.

At first, the old childish delight at seeing the garden and countryside under a blanket of untrodden snow held sway with Sarah. The snowflakes floating so softly past the window often drew her from her desk, half hypnotized, to watch the shrubs disappear into rounded humps, the boughs of the conifers bend with the weight of snow, sometimes precipitating small avalanches when the wind stirred them, the birdbath becoming more and more like a gigantic ice cream cone. When the sun came out, the trees cast steely blue shadows across the snow.

She watched the blackbird who came for the crumbs she threw out, his feathers puffed out for warmth into a round black ball, his orange beak bright against the prevailing whiteness. He was joined by others, robins, starlings, timid thrushes. One morning, on a branch of a hazel tree, a rook huddled with his back to her, looking like a grumpy old man, so still that she thought he must be frozen and had to stay by the window until he moved off in a zig-zag course down the garden, flapping his wings slowly as though stiff, keeping low over the snowy cover looking for food. She would watch until the characters of her book stole into the scene, and she pictured the children's delight in playing in the snow, heard their voices, and was drawn back to her desk.

But after the first few days, the unchanging whiteness began to pall and the inconvenience of getting about began to tell. Clearing the path every day, slithering round the cottage to fetch coal and logs, forging her way to Marlyn Manor, and shopping for Mrs. Pilsen on the way became after the first exhilarating challenge a mere slog, and she longed for the rich variety of nature to emerge from the white blanket which had reduced it all to one sameness. A cold which developed toward the end of the week hastened her disenchantment with the snow, and by the time the wind changed to the kindly southwest and brought a thaw, she was feeling tired and looking, as Paul Rannock put it, decidedly "peaky."

"It's the aftermath of the cold. It was a brute. I usually throw them off much quicker than that."

"I've a suggestion to make, my dear. Simon looked in last night and told me that he was going down to Cornwall next month. Katie has asked him to advise her friend Max on converting an old cottage he's bought down there for a holiday home. Their repertory company is having two months' break while the theater is being decorated and having alterations made to suit new fire regulations, and Katie and Max are going to spend a week or two at a hotel near the cottage. Katie wants Simon to stay on there over Easter. It should be very pleasant in Cornwall in April, and I want you to allow me to give you a little holiday there. Would it appeal?"

"Very much. But . . ."

"No buts. It would be a very small thank you for all you do for me, my dear. And it would please me very much if you would agree."

"How can I refuse, then?" she said, smiling at him. "It's a lovely prospect, and I shall look forward to it. Thank you for thinking of it. But you'll be alone at Easter."

"Alison and Don and Debbie are coming for the weekend, which reminds me to ask you if you'll buy an Easter egg for me for Debbie. A very taking little child, that."

"Of course. Will Simon like the idea? Of me going to Cornwall with him, I mean."

"He thought it a splendid idea. Katie's already booked his accommodation at the hotel, so I shall telephone them this evening and book a room for you. Simon gave me the number. That's settled then. We must hope the sun will shine and bring that sparkle back into your eyes. Now, where were we?"

They resumed work on his memoirs, now well into the last quarter, for he had been working with more urgency lately. Sarah, touched by his kindness, was delighted at the prospect of a spring holiday in Cornwall with Simon, even if his primary object was professional, and as she walked home that evening, conscious of feeling tired, she pictured the Cornish cliffs and coves, anticipated the pleasure of relaxation there in the company of the man who filled her thoughts more and more as the days lengthened and the sun rose higher in the sky.

Her heart lifted as she felt the soft, mild air on her face after the rigors of the past few weeks and saw the catkins on the hazel trees swinging gold above the hedgerow and stopped to feel the furry silvery tufts of the puffy willow, as soft as the fur under Piper's chin. The first tiny leaves starred the hawthorn with green, and she found celandines blooming at the foot of the hedge. No matter what nasty tricks the weather might play, March, she thought, was the month of hope when the country came awake.

It seemed as though Piper shared her mood, for he

leaped out of the hedge as she approached the cottage as though pouncing on prey, stopped suddenly, and butted her legs; then he raced down the lane ahead of her, leaped the gate as though gravity played no part in his life, and chased madly round the lilac tree, stopping suddenly to pat with a gentle, tentative paw something he had seen in the grass. Investigating, Sarah found a small snail. Smiling, she swept Piper up into her arms, where he lay quite peacefully on his back, paws hanging limp, and gazed up at her with limpid green eyes. His mercurial changes of mood never ceased to fascinate her, and the games he played revealed a vivid imagination, which she was sure surpassed that of any other member of his tribe.

"It's spring, Piper," she murmured, laying her cheek against the soft fur of his head as she carried him up the path, "and isn't it a grand and glorious feeling?"

With Piper left to the care of Mrs. Murcia and the garden given over to Jeff Murcia, Sarah packed her case with a blithe heart in the face of Jeff's rather shocked reaction. He could not imagine how any lover of gardens could think of going away at Easter time when there was so much to do and indicated as much to Sarah with a shake of his head and an unspoken reproach in his wizened face. A man of few words, he seemed to have the power of conveying his opinions silently. Sarah got on very well with him and knew that his implied reproach at the thought of anything as frivolous as a holiday was tempered by pleasure at the thought of having the garden to himself over Easter.

They were making an early start for their long drive, and Sarah was waiting at the gate at the appointed time when Simon drove up. It was a fresh, fine morning, the air sweet with the scent of a balsam poplar and the bright new green of spring everywhere.

Simon seemed a little skeptical about the Cornish project.

"I'll know more when I've had a discussion with Max and seen the place. So far, I've only heard Katie's version and you know how she gets carried away. I suspect that it will be a nine days' wonder. The cost of making a primitive cottage into a comfortable retreat with all modern conveniences is usually so much higher than people imagine that they recoil in horror, and I can't see Max happy to rough it. Not the back-to-nature type at all."

"He only wants it for a holiday retreat, though."

"M'm. A discreet hideaway, more likely. Well, we'll see."

"He and Katie? Do you think there's more between them than just a professional partnership?"

"He's not the marrying type, if that's what you mean. And neither, I fancy, is Katie."

Simon, who liked to concentrate on his driving, seemed disinclined to say more, and Sarah was happy to relax and watch the passing scene as they drove westward across an England looking its best in the spring sunshine. Blackthorn was blooming in the hedges, the trees with which the south was so richly endowed were at various stages of leafing, primroses shone from banks, and weeping willows rained ethereal gold. Polyanthuses, wallflowers, and aubrietia had joined the daffodils in country gardens, and the white blossom of wild cherries reminded her of Housman's poem. She feasted her eyes on this pageant with secret joy and gratitude for such bounty.

Simon kept off main roads where possible, which made their journey longer but infinitely more enjoyable. They stopped for a brief lunch at an inn in Dorset, and only the last twisty stretch of narrow

Cornish lanes made them aware that the journey had lasted long enough.

The hotel, which had once been a large country house, was well tucked away off a lane running back from the north Cornish coast and looked inviting as they drove up the graveled drive, its old walled garden colorful, its gray stone walls and mullioned windows forming a pleasing elevation.

"Full marks to Katie. I was wondering what she might have let us in for. The repertory company must be in a more flourishing state than I realized."

Large bowls of daffodils and willow lightened the reception hall with its dark oak paneling and rose-patterned curtains, and they were given a warm welcome at the reception desk. Sarah signed the register and passed the book to Simon without glancing at any other names on the page, but Simon ran his eye upward, and Sarah saw him frown.

"I see we have an additional member to the party. Anna."

Sarah's heart sank as she watched him sign his name.

"Katie didn't mention it?"

"Not a word. This was a business matter, I was given to suppose, involving only Max and me."

And if Simon was surprised to find Anna there, the latter was evidently no less surprised to see Sarah. She came into the lounge where they were sharing a welcome pot of tea after leaving their luggage in their respective rooms, and stopped for a moment when she saw them, not able to hide quickly enough an expression of mingled displeasure and surprise at the sight of Sarah. It was replaced with a charming smile in a moment, though, as she said, "Hello there. Good to see you, Simon! And Sarah, isn't it? Katie didn't tell me you would be here."

"I don't suppose she knew," said Simon. "My

father booked this holiday for Sarah after Katie had fixed a room for me. And she forgot to tell me you would be joining us, too. Life's full of surprises."

"Pleasant ones, I hope. I only decided at the last minute when Katie and Max told me about it and asked me if I'd like to see Max's cottage."

"Well, you're looking as beautiful as ever, Anna. Will you join us for tea or have you had yours?"

"I'll have another with you. A good journey down?"

"Excellent," said Sarah, as Simon signaled the waitress and asked for another cup.

"Have you decided when to return to Italy?" asked Simon.

"Not precisely, but I'll have to go back soon. Business matters connected with the estate are pressing, although my parents want me to stay on a little longer here. You're looking tired, Simon. You work too hard. Come to Italy and stay with us some time this summer. I could teach you how to relax."

Her slow smile was warm, her voice cajoling as she looked at him. She was lying back in the armchair, gracefully indolent. Dressed in a flared skirt of burnt orange with a matching silky sweater and a brown silk scarf knotted at the neck, with her olive complexion and lustrous dark eyes, she seemed to Sarah to convey all the seductive languor of the south, with its philosophy of *mañana,* its sensuous appeal, strikingly at odds with the atmosphere of that very English room on that bright April day. Simon's eyes were lingering on her, and Sarah knew that at that moment she did not exist for either of them, that they were engaged in a secret exchange. Never, she thought, would she see that expression in Simon's eyes for her.

As soon as she could, she made unpacking her excuse to leave them and went upstairs to her room, wondering whether either of them had noticed her going.

She had just finished unpacking, when a sharp

tattoo on the door heralded Katie. She came in, her face sparkling with pleasure.

"A lovely surprise, to have you here, Sarah. Simon should have told me. It was my father's idea, wasn't it?"

"Yes. A kind of bonus for me. Wasn't it kind of him?"

"Very. You've found a soft spot in him that nobody else has."

"How do you know, Katie? You never see him. He's a very kind man, given any encouragement."

"Well, he did without us for so many years. It's a bit late for encouragement now, isn't it? Anyway, it's grand to have you here. I'll be glad of your company because Max is in one of his broody moods and will be concentrating on his cottage. We can explore the coast together. Heavenly coves and cliffs."

"What about Anna? Simon wasn't expecting to find her here."

"Well, I'll let you into it," said Katie confidingly, as she sat on the bed. "Anna is only just starting to get round Simon again. He's proved more stubborn than she expected. She has to return to her home this summer, and we thought this little holiday in Cornwall would provide her with just the right place and time to clinch it. So if you don't mind being saddled with me, we'll leave them to themselves as much as possible."

"I seem to have upset the balance with my intrusion," said Sarah lightly.

"Oh no. Not at all. I'm delighted. Max and I only come to blows if we're together too much. It will work out just fine. I mean, you weren't counting on Simon's company, were you? It was my father's idea and not Simon's?"

"Yes, it was only your father's idea," said Sarah, wondering whether Anna had put Katie up to confirming this.

"Then we'll make ourselves scarce and leave the two love birds to come together, shall we?"

"If that's what they want. Simon seemed to have the idea that he was coming here to sort out Max's requirements for the cottage and advise him on the possibilities."

"Yes, but that won't take long. I found a gorgeous little secret cove yesterday. I must show it to you, Sarah. We could take a picnic lunch one day. I love this wild coast. It will be grand to have Max's cottage available for holiday breaks in future. He wants to make it roomy enough to be able to put up a few friends."

"Sounds a lovely idea."

Katie chattered on for a little about the cottage, then left. Sarah, feeling rather stiff after the long journey, ran a hot bath and soaked in it. Some of the euphoria of the past few days of anticipation had evaporated. The holiday had now taken on a rather different complexion. In spite of Anna's assertion that it had been a last-minute decision to come, Katie had made it obvious that it had been carefully planned between them, and she wondered whether they had made Max's cottage the excuse for fetching Simon here or whether Max had genuinely wanted to consult him and Katie and Anna had merely seized on the opportunity this presented. At least, the past hour or two would seem to suggest that Simon had not changed his position since Christmas, but, recalling that expression in his eyes, she felt that a few days in Anna's company might well shift him. And whatever the outcome, she felt that she was the odd one out, an awkward fifth to two couples.

so much more than that. Look how she worked at Christmas. And it's such a help to Simon to know that she's on hand to keep a watchful eye on his father and let the family know if anything's wrong. He really does value your services highly, Sarah."

"I'm very fond of Paul Rannock," said Sarah quietly, inwardly boiling at Anna's patronizing tone.

"Of course. It's mutual, I believe. It seems a bit hard that Simon isn't free to live his own life, though, in view of the fact that his father ignored the existence of his family all his life until failing health forced him to seek their help."

"Oh, what a glorious sea!" exclaimed Katie, as they came to the cove, and she ran toward the booming rollers as though to embrace them, and Sarah ran with her.

The white, bubbling foam came flooding across the sand to meet them, sparkling in the sunshine. Katie laughed and squealed as she jumped back a foot to escape the wash, picked up a long ribbon of seaweed, called out something to Sarah, which she could not hear above the roar of the waves, and ran along by the edge of the foam, her black hair flying, her face lifted, the ribbon of seaweed held aloft to stream behind her. She was like a child in her joyful abandonment to the here and now, thought Sarah fondly, and was reminded of Piper's rapid responses to the changing moods of the moment. Then she, too, put Anna's wounding remarks out of her mind and ran after Katie, keeping just to the fringe of foam, daring it to reach her as she ran, the salt spray on her face, the smell of seaweed in the air, the wind in her hair, the buoyancy of the sea in her veins.

Simon spent most of that first day at the cottage, taking measurements, making notes. Katie took Sarah off to her secret cove, where they spent a happy hour poking about the rocks, investigating pools, puttering along the edge of the retreating tide, before tackling the steep climb back up the cliff. Gasping, Katie sank down in a grassy hollow as soon as they reached the top.

"Heavens!" she exclaimed, lying flat on her back, "I'm exhausted."

"Isn't that Max with Anna coming along the ridge?" observed Sarah when they had regained their breath.

Katie sat up and confirmed it. They were walking arm in arm, and as they came to a clump of stunted trees, stopped. Sarah could see the red glint of Anna's pants-suit through the branches. Katie chuckled.

"Trust Maxie to offer consolation for Simon's absence."

"Is he a candidate, too, then?"

"Max is always happy to comfort an attractive female, and Anna's rather special, after all. Simon had better not overdo the hard-to-get role. Not that Anna has eyes for anybody else, really. It's an obsession with her. She told me that she thought about him every single day and night after their break."

"Hard luck on her husband," said Sarah drily.

"Well, that was a marriage of convenience. Ah, back to business," added Katie, as Max and Anna emerged from the trees and continued their walk, heads close together. "Max has hopes of Anna backing a company of his own he wants to form. To be an actor-manager is Max's aim. Anna's very interested in the theater, and if and when she marries Simon, they'd spend a good deal of time over here. Anna's parents are here, and Simon would want to keep in touch with the family, although we're so tiresome. This venture rather appeals to her, and of course she's got pots of money to play with."

"There's a hawk," exclaimed Sarah, watching the bird hovering high above them.

But Katie was not interested in birds, and she jumped up.

"Let's catch them," she said, and began to take the downward slope of the grassy cliff-top at a run.

Sarah watched the hawk swoop, strike, and soar upward again within the space of a second or two. She thought it was a kestrel and guessed that a field mouse had met its end. A cry drew her eyes away from the sky. Katie was half lying on the grassy slope, holding her ankle.

"A rabbit hole I didn't see," she said, her face twisted with pain, as Sarah ran up. "I think I've sprained my ankle."

Leaning on Sarah's arm, she tested it out gingerly but could take no weight on it.

"We'll need another strong arm to help you home. I'll get Max," said Sarah, and ran off, leaving Katie nursing her ankle.

Max and Anna had reached the end of the ridge and were now taking the beach-way back to the hotel. It was low tide, and the sand was firm beneath her feet as she ran after them. They disappeared around a rocky headland and Sarah, slowing down for lack of breath, found when she approached the headland that they had stopped just the other side, for their words came clearly to her; Max's well-produced voice made him seem at her elbow.

"You don't think that girl's causing any diversion?"

"Who? Sarah? Oh no. She's useful to him for taking on some of the responsibility for his father. To Simon, she's a nice child whose help is welcome. No more. Believe me, Max, there's only one woman on Simon's mind, and that's me. I know."

"On his mind? Elsewhere, too, I fancy."

"It's maddening of him to play coy like this, but I

do believe he's enjoying it. Making me pay a little. Well, I'm willing. But not for much longer."

"You really do have a grand passion for him, don't you? With your equipment, Anna, you must have a wide choice, and I'm surprised you don't leave him to stew."

"Cynical Max. There never was anybody else for me and never will be. I want him and don't mean to lose him again."

"Well, good hunting, my dear. Call me in if you need a rehearsal. I'll understudy him quite happily."

Anna laughed and their voices receded. Sarah waited a few moments, then walked round the headland and shouted. They stopped and turned, and she ran along the beach to them.

"Katie's twisted her ankle. Could you come back and give her a hand, Max? She'll need two of us to get her back to the hotel."

"Trust Katie!" said Max resignedly. "What an accident-prone creature she is!"

Between them they managed to get Katie back to the hotel, where cold compresses were applied to her ankle before Sarah bandaged it firmly for support.

Katie's mishap kept her more or less confined to the hotel and its garden during the next two days. She could hobble with the aid of a stick, and Sarah kept her company a good deal of the time while Anna attached herself to Simon with a persistence that in another woman might have seemed crass but which Anna managed with a diplomatic charm that could not be faulted.

Simon himself puzzled Sarah. Beneath his customary easy assurance, she sensed a tension without being able to guess at its cause and nature. Was it a state of triumphant love masked for the benefit of onlookers or was it a state of anger that put that gleam in his dark eyes and fired him with a restless energy, as though he could barely control some force within himself? He was certainly riding with a tight rein on something, she thought, and although his manner remained easy and controlled with the others, on the few occasions when they were alone together, he did not seem to feel any mask necessary and remained either preoccupied or definitely snappish.

To add to her discomfort, Sarah found that when she left Katie to her own devices, Max was apt to appear at her side and offer his company. She could only presume that he had taken over the task of watchdog to see that she did not encroach on the intimacy of Anna and Simon, and his attentions both irritated and in an odd way humiliated her. His flirtatious attitude was meant, she supposed, to be flattering. A green girl being given the attentions of the glamorous actor for a treat. And when this state of affairs brought a brotherly word of advice from Simon, her own temper was as short as his.

"You want to watch your step with Max, Sarah," he said on one of the rare occasions when they were alone in the hotel garden.

"What do you mean?" she asked coolly.

"That he's too experienced to be satisfied with party games. You might get more than you bargain for."

"How old do you think this simpleton is?" she demanded, her anger, fired by the humiliations and disappointment of this Easter holiday, shooting up like a rocket.

"It's not a question of years," he replied shortly. "I'm just warning you."

"Keeping a big-brotherly eye on me? I'll tell Max next time I see him that he's much too dangerous to be alone with, shall I?"

"No need to be so bad-tempered. I'm only pointing out that Max is a wolf, and his idea of play can be rough."

"What with female maneaters and male wolves, one might think we were on safari," she snapped.

And then his eyes crinkled up and she saw the absurdity of it and could not help laughing with him.

"That was quite witty of you," he observed. "What's biting you?"

What was biting her, she thought unhappily. She was in love with a man who insisted on treating her like a child. That was what was biting her.

"Nothing worth discussing," she said. "And I might ask what is biting you? You've been snapping at me like a dog at a bee when we've been alone."

"Have I? Well, I have problems and I lack your kind nature, Sarah. Don't see why you should object to my giving you a friendly warning about Max, though."

Exasperated again, she tried to control her tongue. It wasn't his fault if he saw her still as the child, Sarah Rushden, who used to be one of the tiresome family he had to keep an eye on.

"Should people in glass houses throw stones?" she asked mildly enough.

"Come clear." His eyes held a warning glint, but she was not in a cautious mood.

"Your own affairs are scarcely so well organized as to inspire confidence in your role as adviser," she said crisply.

"I wish you wouldn't talk like a lecturer at a literary society meeting. It's most irritating."

"Anything is irritating to bear with a sore head."

"For heaven's sake! You're the touchy one. I merely remarked that Max is a womanizer, and if you go off for long solitary walks with him, he'll have other things in mind than the lovely scenery. And you might not like it."

"And why not?"

"Because you're a romantic and could easily come a cropper with a man like Max."

"By romantic, you mean a fool? Arrested development?"

"No. I mean someone with ideals but little worldly experience."

"Anyone would think I'd lived in a convent to hear you talk. I've earned my own living in London since I was seventeen, remember? I've held a responsible job and met quite a variety of males in the course of it. I know very well what sort of man Max Raigarth is, and I don't need your doubtless well-meant warnings."

"Does your conversation always mount these stilts when you're in a bad temper? If you enjoy Max's flattering attentions, go ahead. And pay the bill."

"I do not enjoy his attentions," she said, her anger out of control now. "They are forced on me because Katie, who was to have been my watchdog to keep me from intruding on the 'love birds'—I use Katie's words—is more or less out of action. So Max has taken over."

She had done it now. Simon's face was white with anger and as grim as the granite cliffs.

"Just enlarge on that, will you?" he said icily.

"Certainly. My arrival was both unexpected and awkward because I would be the odd one out. So, rather than be a spoilsport, I was asked by Katie to leave you and Anna to yourselves. In order to make certain that I did so, Max took over Katie's watchdog duties."

"And why should Max care?"

"Presumably because he wants to keep in Anna's good grace because she is considering putting up some capital, entering into some sort of partnership with him so that he can form his own company of players. He wants to keep her interest here in

England as well as in Italy, and you would help to do that if you would kindly stop playing hard-to-get and marry Anna, as you once wished to do, and still do, according to Katie and Anna."

"You must have enjoyed all these cozy chats about my affairs."

"No. I've merely been the victim. Irrelevant but getting in the way. So I have to put up with Max. And if I'd known what the situation was, I would never have come."

"The situation was not of my making," he said bitterly. "Katie again. A repeat of the Christmas surprise. I'll sort that girl out once and for all."

"Don't blame Katie. You say I'm a romantic. It's Katie who's the romantic. Anna planned it with her, but Katie truly believes that you love Anna and that by bringing you together she's doing you a good turn."

"Rubbish! She's enamoured of Anna's wealth and position and that villa in Italy. She would love to have Anna for a sister-in-law."

"That's partly the reason for her interest, but she does truly believe that you love Anna. Perhaps Anna has convinced her of that. And as you reveal nothing of your feelings yourself, she has only Anna's word to go on."

"Why should I blab to all and sundry about my personal affairs?"

"No reason at all. But unfortunately, Anna doesn't share your reticence, so the picture comes from one side only. And the fact that you were both passionately in love a few years ago was well known, after all."

"It's an intolerable situation. I'll not have Katie interfering in this way. I begin to wonder whether Max really wanted to consult me about that cottage. I bet when I let him have a specification and estimate, he'll turn it down as too expensive, having known all along that it would be. I dislike being made a fool of."

She saw that he was being rubbed raw by the situation, and her own anger subsided. To have his most intimate affairs the subject of discussion and plotting among outsiders would rile a far more stolid man than Simon.

"Are you sure about your own feelings?" she asked gently.

He looked at her for a moment, then put a hand on her shoulder.

"Yes, and I'm not proud of them. It's all very complex. But I'm sorry your holiday has been spoiled by all this. You needn't have been so cross because I offered a bit of advice, though, even if it was unnecessary. You shouldn't spit in the face of the wind," he added with a wry smile.

"I don't like being treated as a child."

"And so you react childishly. Foolish. We know each other too well for such pantomimes. I don't think you're a child. In some ways, I think you're a very wise person. You have a sound sense of values and a simplicity which is your strength. And I don't have to tell the expert on words that simplicity and simpleton are not the same. Is that soothing ointment?"

She nodded, giving him a wan smile.

"But sex is a difficult passion to handle," he said to Sarah. "Sensuality an insidious weapon. I thought that in that field you weren't too well prepared. That its earthier aspects were outside your experience."

"All right. You win," Sarah said quietly. For how could she tell him that she ached to feel his arms around her, that frustration and unhappiness at the situation between him and Anna, with all its uncertainties and contradictions, caused her heart to ache as painfully as his at this moment.

And Anna's insinuation that he kept her around

for convenience, false though she felt it was, still galled her as though it were a blatant denial of her identity.

"Well, tomorrow we'll try to organize something we can all enjoy."

"I doubt if that will be possible with this disparate party," she said, feeling that he was patting her on the head again.

And at that juncture, Anna came down the steps of the terrace and joined them. She tucked her arm in Simon's with a smile.

"You promised you'd have a look at my windshield wiper, Simon. The weather forecast is poor for tomorrow and I may need to use it, so will you see if you can do anything with it?"

"Things shouldn't go wrong on that expensive car of yours," he replied, and they walked off together toward the car park behind the hotel.

Sarah watched them, a chill feeling in her heart. Anna tall, with a long-limbed grace, but Simon topping her by a few inches. Her smooth black hair was coiled at the nape of her neck, and her slim-cut black trousers and jade green silk top might have been specially designed to show off every curve of her body. Simon, tanned to a darker complexion even than usual by the outdoor activities of the past days, was wearing a brown terry sportshirt with fawn slacks.

She saw them for that moment of time as though they were two strangers. A striking, well-matched couple. How did Anna manage to keep every hair smooth and in place even while Cornish breezes were blowing? Plastered with lacquer, she supposed. There were a few people whose appearance never seemed subject to the same stresses and strains as that of ordinary people. Their clothes remained uncreased after the longest journeys, their makeup was never less than immaculate, their poise never seemed threatened. And she saw then how, beside Anna, she must appear to Simon as unsophisticated as a schoolgirl, subject to fractious moods, needing to be patted on the head sometimes after a little lesson. Which was doubtless why he never revealed his deepest feelings to her. She was no wiser now than she had been at the beginning of their discussion about his relationship with Anna. She only knew that some sort of battle was going on between them, and she thought that Anna in the end was likely to win.

CHAPTER THIRTEEN

SARAH WOKE UP the next morning to rain, and from the uniform grayness of the sky, it looked as though it had come to stay for some time.

After breakfast, they sat in the lounge reading the papers. As the morning progressed, Anna embarked on a game of patience; Katie started to read through her part in the next play. Max sought refuge in a paperback while Simon remained resolutely buried behind *The Times*. Sarah, seized with a sudden fit of restlessness, decided that she would deck herself out for the rain and go for a walk. It was an idea which had no appeal, apparently, to the others. Simon merely lowered his paper and raised an incredulous eyebrow before returning to whatever it was he was engrossed in. Anna carried on with her patience without comment, Katie, looking out of the window, said she'd brought no oilskins with her, and Max said, "And the best of luck, my dear."

Once outside, her raincoat buttoned up, a rainproof scarf tied round her head, she felt better, even if the landscape had all but vanished behind a wet gray mist. Whether her nerves were unduly sensitive she did not know, but it had seemed to her that there had been an uneasy atmosphere among their party that morning from which she was glad to escape. She started along the track up to the headland, but the wind in her face was too fierce and threatened to drench her within minutes, so she retreated back to the lane and walked along it, protected a little by the tall hedges, past the hotel and on toward a crossroad where she had noticed a cottage advertising teas and coffees.

She had just ordered a cup of coffee and some hotcakes from a buxom little white-haired woman when a car drew up outside. Then Max came into the room, stooping his head under the low lintel of the door, seeming to dwarf the little sitting room with its old-fashioned furniture and crowded ornaments.

"Thought it was you ahead of me," he said with a smile. "Can I join you? God, what a morning!"

"I'm surprised that you ventured out."

"Saw a card on the hotel notice board advertising an art exhibition at a little place along the coast. Local artists. Thought I'd like to have a look at it. Might pick something up for the cottage. Find hotel lounges on a wet day a bit dismal."

He ordered coffee and looked round him, rubbing his hands. They were the only two people there.

"You couldn't persuade Katie to come with you? It's tiresome for her to be so bogged down with that ankle."

"No, she's immersed in *Twelfth Night*, and has taken it off to her room."

"She'll make a good Viola, I imagine."

"Yes."

"Do you do many classics?"

"No. One, perhaps two, in a mixed repertory season."

"How do you rate Katie as an actress? She seems to me to have great potential, with her looks and imagination and vivid personality."

"Come and see us and find out. We're based at a theater in Surrey this year. Not so far to come."

"But I lack transport. I'd be interested in your professional opinion, though."

He sugared his coffee and stirred it thoughtfully.

"Katie's good. She will be better. It's a tough struggle for recognition in our profession, but she and I will make it. Are beginning to make it."

"Your aim is to be actor-manager of a company of your own, Katie tells me."

"Yes. Capital's the problem. But I intend to do it, some time. Then I can put Katie in the right parts. And myself."

"You see yourself as a team, then?"

"Katie needs me. Needs guidance. Besides, she has star quality, and I can give that star the chance to twinkle."

He would, too, thought Sarah. There was a single-minded determination there. A powerful force. An Irving? Or a Svengali? And as a team, she could see how well they would offset each other. Katie with her wild grace, her vivacity, and Max powerful, with an almost menacing force, a presence nobody could ignore.

"It sounds a very exciting prospect. I wish you luck."

"Thanks. We shall need it. We're bedevilled with economics. But you, Sarah. You say remarkably little about yourself. Just observe us all with thoughtful brown eyes. Gathering material for your books?"

"I write for children."

"Why?"

"Because I enjoy it. Because, perhaps, I find the adult world too complex to write about. I find it easier to put myself into the mind of a child, remembering my own childhood."

"And you really like living on your own in a cottage and gardening and going for long solitary walks, Katie tells me. An escapist?"

"The reverse. I live a life which has reality for me. Grassroots. When I worked in London, it all seemed artificial, meaningless."

When he chose, she thought, he could be sympathetic enough. She glanced out of the window. The rain was sheeting down, blotting out everything.

"You can't walk back in this," said Max. "Why not come along with me to the art exhibition? Better than killing time in the hotel lounge waiting for lunch."

After a moment's hesitation, she agreed, thinking that it would pass an hour agreeably enough, but after half an hour's drive through torrential rain, it occurred to her that the little place along the coast was farther than he had given her to understand.

"Where is this place?" she asked.

"Penstow."

"I thought it was only a few miles."

"M'm. It's farther than I realized. I had a glance at the map, but these twisting lanes make distances twice as far as they look."

"At this rate, we shan't be able to get back for lunch."

"Does that worry you? We can get lunch on the road or at Penstow."

"I left the hotel for a short walk. Don't want Simon sending out search parties when I don't turn up for lunch."

"We'll telephone at the first phone. Can you see what that signpost says?"

"Penstow to the right," she said, peering through the rain.

"In any case," said Max casually as he took the bend, "I don't think Simon will worry because when I left he and Anna were talking of going into Truro for lunch. Anna wants to do some shopping and the windshield wiper on her car has broken, so Simon's obliging. They thought they might make an evening of it, if Truro has any shows that appeal."

There was nothing to be done, she thought, but relax and make the best of it, although she would not have chosen to spend the day with Max. She wondered whether it was all as casual as it seemed, though. Max was too experienced a motorist not to assess mileage accurately from a map.

It turned out to be just over an hour's drive to Penstow, a pretty little fishing village huddled round a cove, which they reached after a tortuous descent down a narrow, twisting road. They had lunch at the small inn there, which offered them good hot soup, crusty French bread and cheese, and coffee. A cheerful fire was burning in the small lounge bar where they sat, and they had it to themselves while the rain continued to fall pitilessly, as though determined to wash everything away.

Over lunch, Max talked about the theater, told her amusing tales of disasters on tour, and proved more agreeable than at any time before. He had dropped the flirtatious manner, which had so irritated her during the past two days, and seemed willing to meet her on her own ground, realizing, perhaps, that she was not vulnerable to his charms. It was his pale gray eyes that disturbed her; there was a chilling, assessing quality about them. Those and the sensual curve of the mouth. He could be cruel, she thought. But perhaps he was just not her type. Katie seemed to have established a good working relationship with him, quite unabashed.

The exhibition, held in a small hall halfway up the main street, surprised her with its quality. The paintings were mostly of Cornish sea and landscapes, but the one which Max finally chose to buy was an oil painting of a market square, with shop fronts, barrows, people, a dog. It was full of life and color. Her own first choice fell on a painting of a ridge, with a stream running down to the sea, and an old stone church just visible among the trees at the top. The colors were soft, autumnal, and captured a gentler aspect than usual of the Cornish landscape. But she had no money to spare for pictures.

Max, who had taken a long time studying the

pictures, now entered into a leisurely conversation with the man in charge of the exhibition. Max, it seemed, was knowledgeable about this branch of the arts. Then he wrote out a check and arranged to pick up the picture when the exhibition closed at the end of the week.

They stopped for a pot of tea on their way back and found on emerging from the cottage that the rain had lessened to a fine drizzle, and a thin streak of sun could be seen in the west below the gray pall of cloud. When their road brought them close to the coast, Max said, "A rough sea. Let's go down here and have a look at it."

He turned down a narrow track and drew up on a grassy patch from which they had a view of the sea-lashed cliffs. It was high tide, and although the wind which had been driving the rain now seemed to have subsided, the sea was broken with white horses and the waves thudded against the base of the cliffs, sending up showers of spray like billowing white veils. As Sarah looked down at it, she felt Max's arm around her waist, and was drawn closer.

"An enjoyable day salvaged from the rain. Thank you, Sarah."

"Your doing, not mine," she said lightly.

"A hint of *double entendre* there, I fancy. You know, you intrigue me, Sarah. Your looks are so inviting. Warm coloring, a generous mouth, soft eyes. But always, the gap. An unobtrusive withdrawal. From me, at least."

"Should four days' acquaintance have made us closer, then? How frightening, to be out on that sea."

"Time is too short to be dilatory. Come closer, my dear. I don't bite."

His hand was wandering in places not to her liking and she removed it, remembering with an amused little twitch of her lips Simon's remark about Max not being concerned with lovely scenery.

The hand, however, was now holding her chin, pulling her face round to make her look at him. She did not much care for his expression. He liked a little opposition, she guessed.

"Is it unreasonable to expect a thank you for being saved the excruciating boredom of a wet day in the hotel?"

"I might have preferred a little trip to Truro," she said sweetly, "but I did quite enjoy the exhibition, so thank you, Max. Shall we get back to the hotel now?"

"You wouldn't have been welcome on that trip, my dear, and you're too sensitive not to know it. And I'd like a rather warmer thank you before we go back. Don't tell me you're not capable of improving on that chilly effort."

"I'm afraid I have to tell you so." She considered him gravely. "I'm sorry. Something wrong with the chemistry. You must find me an oddity, I'm sure. But it can't be helped."

"You're too smart with words, my lady. I'm going to stop your mouth."

He had moved over and had her across his lap. His mouth was soft and probing on hers. She refused to struggle, realizing that that would please him, and in any case knowing that he was too strong for her. She lay there passively, trying not to flinch from his roving hand, enduring his searching lips on hers. Her limp passivity had the desired effect.

"So you're not playing?"

"Definitely not."

"I could go on."

"No fun without any response. Except for rapists, of course."

"Clever girl," he said ironically, but he released her.

"Shall we go back to the hotel now?" she asked politely, smoothing her skirt.

He said nothing while he lit a cigarette. As she watched him, he looked up and a wry smile drove the anger from his face.

"If I had more time, Miss Play-It-Cool, I'd enjoy laying siege to you and getting a sizzling surrender."

They drove the last mile back to the hotel in a state of not inharmonious truce.

"It doesn't look as though Anna found any show appealing," said Sarah, as Simon's car turned into the drive of the hotel just ahead of them.

As they drew up, Anna emerged from Simon's car, slammed the door, and ran into the hotel without a glance for anybody. It did not suggest a happy day out. Sarah slid out of the car and Max drove it around to the parking area behind the hotel. Simon had not emerged from his car, and when Sarah walked up, she found him leaning on the steering wheel, staring grimly ahead and looking so exhausted that the words of greeting died on her lips.

She said, "You look tired out, Simon. Anything wrong?"

"Emotional scenes are tiring and I've had many today. I wish you hadn't opted to spend the day with Max instead of coming to Truro. I needed a buffer."

"I really didn't have any option, and I knew nothing about the proposed trip to Truro until it was too late."

"I was afraid of that when Max telephoned." He passed a hand wearily over his eyes, then added abruptly, "It promises to be a fine sunset. Care to walk down to the cove with me? I could do with some fresh air and your sane company."

"Give me five minutes to change my shoes. These are still damp."

"I'll wait for you at the gate."

The clouds had broken up and raindrops winked at them like diamonds from the bushes as they walked down the lane toward the sea. The air was sweet and fresh after the rain, and only a gentle breeze remained from the strong southwest wind of the day. The sea was foam-flecked and turbulent still, and the sky streaked with pink and gold as the sun dipped to the horizon. Sarah waited for Simon to speak, content to be silent if he wished. When they reached the cove, which was only a few minutes' walk from the hotel, he suggested that they climb up the far headland for a wider view.

"Unless you're tired," he added.

"No. I've been sitting in a car most of the day. I'd like the climb."

"What happened? We saw you walk back past the hotel this morning, and at that stage, we'd all decided to spend the day in Truro, knowing that you'd be back shortly. Max said he wanted to get some gas and he'd look out for you, as the rain was belting down harder than ever. The next thing, he telephoned to say he'd noticed this art exhibition advertised at the reception desk and that you'd both decided you'd prefer that to Truro and were on your way. At which news, Katie begged off and decided to stick to studying her part. What actually happened?"

She told him, concluding lightly, "I was conned, you might say, but quite enjoyed the exhibition. A smooth operator, is Max."

"Any trouble?"

"Not that I couldn't handle."

He smiled then, and said, "I'll learn not to worry about you in time, I dare say."

"Were you worried?"

"A bit bothered, say. They work well together, those three. Katie, Anna, and Max."

"Would you rather cut the holiday short and go back tomorrow?"

"That won't really solve it, my dear."

"I don't know exactly what the situation is between

you and Anna, Simon, but it's obviously wearing you to shreds. There must be a solution."

They had reached the end of the cove and stopped at the foot of the path up the headland to look back along the coast. The tide was falling now, but the wash of the waves was loud in their ears. The sky had taken on richer tones, and a group of gulls winging across the bay seemed to have caught some of the colors in their wings. Their plaintive, mewing cries receded as Simon climbed up on to the path and gave her a hand. It was a steady pull up the trail, and they said no more until they reached the top, where they stopped to lean on the back of a seat to survey the splendor of that stormy sunset.

"It helps to get the perspective right," said Simon, after they had spent a few minutes in silent tribute to that glorious ending to the wet and dismal day.

"That's what I always find."

"Tell me, Sarah. Supposing you were in love with a man who no longer loved you and you thought that all his efforts to make you believe that the old love had perished were merely a punishment for past betrayal, after which all would be as before. Is there anything that would finally convince you that for him the past was dead and buried? Because I'm defeated. Plain words don't seem enough."

"Plain words for me would be enough. But for Anna . . . I don't know. Can you tell me more about it? If things went so deep with both of you and lasted for a long time, it might be hard to believe that it could die."

"I can't tell you more about it. It seems indecent, somehow, to discuss old loves. I can only put the proposition to you. What would convince you finally if you can imagine yourself in that position? I begin to feel that the female mind is beyond my rational comprehension. Perhaps you can enlighten me. I've been brutally frank, have never wavered since Anna turned up in my life again last Christmas. But she telephones me constantly, at my flat, at Marlyn Manor, at the office. She waits outside my flat or office, she pleads, rages, and humiliates herself in a way I find quite unbearable. She's sure I'm punishing her for marrying someone else but that underneath, when I'm satisfied that she's paid enough, I'll let her make up for everything. And what sort of a sadist I'd have to be to play like that is neither here nor there. That's what she truly believes. So, if you were Anna, what could I do that would convince you that it was all over?"

Sarah thought for a few minutes, then said carefully, "I think that the only way to convince Anna, because that's the way she is, would be to prove that your love had turned elsewhere."

"How prove? Anna wouldn't take my word for it."

"Something official. An engagement."

"Yes," said Simon slowly. "I see the force of that. But it's scarcely practical, is it? How can I rustle up a candidate for that?"

"I'll take on the part, if you like. In a few months' time, after Anna's returned to her home in Italy, we could announce quietly that it had been a mistake."

"I couldn't involve you in that sort of pretense, Sarah."

"It wouldn't hurt anybody. We would be the only people to know the true nature of the bargain. It's a crazy solution, perhaps, but it's a crazy situation, and it's wearing you out. Obsessions can't be cured rationally. That's the only thing I can suggest."

"I don't like using you, Sarah. I'm very fond of you, as you must know. I respect you. I can't make use of you."

"I make the offer, gladly. I'm not committed to anyone else. It can do no harm."

"I think we'd both better think this over tonight.

Remember, you'll be involved in pretense. My father, for example, would be delighted. You're not a person for sham, Sarah. It could make you feel uncomfortable. Me, too."

"As uncomfortable as the present situation is making you?"

"Nothing could be as uncomfortable as that. It's as bad as anything in Dante's *Inferno*."

His profile against the darkening sky revealed a gauntness more marked than she had seen before. Remembering what Katie had told her, she felt appalled at the havoc Anna had wreaked in his life over the past five years and more. Anna, a passionate woman, doubtless thrived on dramatic, emotional scenes, but to Simon they were anathema. She knew him now to be a man of deep feeling but controlled, reserved, and the last person to thrive on histrionics. She felt that he had reached the limits of endurance, and desperate measures were called for.

"I understand your scruples, and I share them up to a point," she said gently, "but don't you see, Simon, it's just because we are such good friends and trust each other that such a bargain is possible. I don't want to try to persuade you against your better judgment, of course. But I can't think of any other remedy to cut through this entanglement."

He turned then and, taking her face between his hands, scrutinized it with an intensity that was searing, as though he looked into her heart and mind and no secrets were hidden from him. She never forgot that moment. It was imprinted in her memory forever. Simon's dark face against the flaming pageant of the sky, the sound of the sea below, the plaintive cry of a gull above them as, very gently, he kissed her, and said with an odd smile, "For old times' sake?"

She nodded, speechless. With his arm around her shoulder, they stood watching the sky as the colors deepened until only a dark crimson streak on the western horizon remained before night took over and the first stars appeared between the clouds.

Simon broke the silence.

"We're going to be very late for dinner unless we move fast. We'll think it over tonight, my dear, and talk about it again tomorrow. Before the conspirators at the hotel can trap us again, I suggest that you and I go off early tomorrow morning and escape for the day. How about a trip to the Scillies? We must salvage something from this holiday, and if we leave at half-past seven, we can catch the nine-thirty boat across. What do you say?"

"Sounds a splendid idea."

"It's about time we indulged in a little conspiracy of our own."

Only on the last stretch up the lane did Sarah realize how tired she felt. It had been a taxing day.

CHAPTER FOURTEEN

IT WAS MISTY when they drove away from the hotel the next morning, but by the time they reached Penzance, the sun had broken through and the day promised to be fine. As though the stormy weather of the previous day had been a dream, the sea sparkled placidly with not a whitecap to be seen.

She could not tell from Simon's manner what he had decided to do, and she left it to him to bring up the subject, content to be alone with him, free from the pressures of the others. Whatever might be said about the rest of their small party, none of them was exactly restful, she thought. Max, Katie, Anna. All of them demanding in their different ways.

They found a quiet spot near the stern of the boat as they left Penzance behind them and headed westward along the Cornish coast. The Easter holiday was over and the boat was not crowded. The sun was warm on their faces as they leaned on the rail.

"Penny for them," said Simon after a while.

"I was thinking how restful it was to be away from the others. The quiet life for me, every time."

"You can say that again."

"They won't be very pleased."

"Time they forgot their respective egoisms. Katie will doubtless revert to her childish habit of refusing to speak to me and looking all tragic and hurt like Ophelia when she's read the note I pushed under her door this morning."

"Sometimes, when she was a child, it was more like the shrew when she was crossed, I remember."

"M'm. She's given that up in favor of tragedy lately. It doesn't usually last long, though. Liveliness keeps breaking through."

"Dear Katie. I hope you weren't too hard on her."

"Just to the point. Willful brat."

"So much imagination. That's what makes her a good actress, I suppose. Max thinks she'll really reach the top."

"Could be. Have you thought over all the implications of what you suggested last night?"

"Yes."

"And?"

"The offer's still open."

A man had come and joined them, leaning on the rail a few feet away.

"I want to change it a little, but we'll discuss that later. What about a coffee?"

Sarah warmed to the Scillies from the first sight of the small group of islands smiling under the blue sky of that April day. After the *Scillonian* had docked at St. Mary's, they found that the sea trip had given them a good appetite, and they had an early lunch straight away at a restaurant on the jetty, sitting by a window which gave them a view across the harbor, with its colorful launches and sailing boats riding at anchor, an air of sunny somnolence hanging over the small stone houses and unobtrusive hotels during that lunch hour.

"We've only got a few hours here, so there's no point in rushing round trying to see more than a corner. What would you like to concentrate on?" asked Simon.

"The walk round the headland we passed in the boat. It looked so inviting. In fact, it all looks inviting. I wish we'd come for a week."

"There will be other times," he said, smiling at her enthusiasm. "It doesn't take you long to decide that you like a place."

"First impressions seldom prove false, I've found. A question of being in tune with a place. I feel that the Scillies are in my key. No grandeur, no formality, no traffic. Just sunshine and sea and ... Well, let's go and explore," she said, unwilling to spend another moment over coffee.

One of the most vivid recollections she carried back with her of those few hours on St. Mary's was the brilliance of the evergreen shrubs, so thickly covered in bloom that scarcely a green needle could be seen—and it's heady scent.

"It's like coconut. A special, heavenly kind of coconut," she said.

A few early bluebells were pushing through the bracken each side of their footpath, and white flowers of garlic mingled there, too. They came out to smooth, grassy slopes broken up by huge granite boulders, and after they had been walking for some time, Simon said, "Here's a comfortable patch with a good backrest. Let's sit down for a bit."

Sarah, wary after the previous day's experience, had brought her raincoat, and using this and Simon's windbreaker to sit on, they leaned against the granite boulder, warmed by the sun, the sea a sparkling blue beneath them.

"About our engagement, Sarah," said Simon, lighting a cigarette. "The only terms on which I'll accept your offer are if it's not a sham. I'm not going to involve you in a charade, in pretense and deception, just to get me out of an awkward situation."

She turned to him, eyes wide with surprise, questioning. He was gazing out to sea, frowning, and it was a few moments before he went on.

"I said yesterday that I couldn't discuss my love affair with Anna; such things are private. But if I'm asking you to marry me, you have a right to know where I stand now. I put so much into that affair. No, that's not quite accurate. I was so deeply involved, I got so badly mauled, that I emerged completely burned out. The ashes are quite cold. Could never be rekindled. But there are different kinds of loving. I'm very fond of you, Sarah. I care about your happiness. I think we could be happy together, if that is enough for you. Last night, I felt that you ... might care for me, too."

So, she thought, he had read what was in her heart, although she had never meant him to. She looked down, confused and uncertain. Nearby, a bumblebee was busy among a cluster of violets. It went from flower to flower, bending each down with its heavy embrace. Simon's hand turned her face to his.

"Will you marry me, Sarah?"

She was silent for some time, then she said, quietly, "If you feel the same at the end of the summer, Simon, I will."

"Why not now?"

"Because I'd like you to have time to get over this painful experience of Anna's return, in case your proposal is just a rebound from that, and you might feel differently once she's gone back to Italy and left you free. You've been caught in so many bonds to other people. I'd hate you to feel bound to me just because I suggested the engagement as a way of escape for you."

"You're too scrupulous, and I do know my own mind."

"But the suggestion came from me. It would never have entered your head before last night."

"There comes a time when you see things more clearly."

"Shall we agree to a trial engagement, to be confirmed at the end of the summer? That will get rid of any element of sham, will free you from Anna, and give us both time to confirm what has been, after all, a very hasty decision."

"If that is what you wish, so be it. On the first day of September, then, it shall be confirmed. Let me try to reassure you for a start."

He took her in his arms and ran his fingers down her cheek before kissing her. When she responded, he drew her closer, saying, before he kissed her again, "My dear, honest Sarah."

Simon insisted on going through the town to see if he could buy a ring to mark the engagement, and they found in a jeweler's shop a little heart-shaped amethyst in an antique filigree setting which appealed to Sarah. It fitted her engagement finger perfectly, and with the warm good wishes of the shopkeeper following them, they had to hurry back to the boat, whose warning whistle had sounded some time before.

"I shall always love this place," said Sarah, as they leaned on the rail and watched the ropes being cast off.

"We'll come back. For our honeymoon, perhaps."

This idyllic mood lasted until they were in sight of Penzance harbor, when Simon became briskly practical.

"We'll leave for home early tomorrow morning. It's a long drive, and in any case, I don't want you exposed to Anna for long. She has claws."

"Katie's going to be disappointed, too. And

Max. For different reasons. I don't think, somehow, we're going to get any warm congratulations."

"We can put out our own flags. We shall be late in to dinner, anyway. They may not have waited. So we won't have to put up with their various disappointments for long."

The others had not waited for them and had reached the coffee stage by the time Sarah and Simon arrived together in the diningroom. Simon had waited for her in the hall and gave her a reassuring smile as he said, "You look rather too much like a lamb being led to the slaughter."

"Not at all. Just saving my victory smile for the right moment."

"That's my girl. You have a delightful sense of humor. That's why it's going to be so agreeable to live with you. No passionate scenes. No tearful reproaches. No emotional blackmail. Just that impish light in your eyes and a few well chosen words to put me in my place."

"That will be the day."

"Ready to face the music?"

"Yes."

Three pairs of eyes watched them with various degrees of curiosity as Simon saw Sarah seated and then said, "Sorry we're late. I was hoping you might have waited to share some champagne with us, but as it scarcely goes well with coffee, Sarah and I will have to indulge on our own."

Anna, her dark eyes stormy, was watching Simon intently. Max was holding his chin and eyeing Sarah in a speculative manner. It was Katie who spoke with an injured air, and her customary indiscretion.

"Since you indicated in the note you left me that you wanted no more of our company, why should you expect us to wait dinner for you?"

"Did I do that?" said Simon innocently. "Very

boorish of me. My only excuse is that I'd been trying to be alone with Sarah ever since we arrived, and somehow I've never managed it until today."

"And why was that so important?" demanded Katie.

Sarah saw Simon's lips twitch. He had known that Katie would do it for him.

"Well, I wanted to ask her to marry me, but it's a bit embarrassing to do it in public," he said blandly.

Katie spluttered over her coffee. Anna looked at Simon incredulously. Max said calmly, "And did she say yes?"

"Happily for me."

"Well, congratulations." Max's sardonic tone hardly matched his words.

"Sarah!" exclaimed Katie reproachfully. "You led me up the garden path."

Anna now broke her silence as she stood up, her face frightening in its suppressed fury and malevolence. She had her voice under control, however, as she said icily, "What a convenient arrangement for you, Simon," and walked out, as though at any second her control would break.

"Well, I don't understand," said Katie, "but I wish you both all the happiness in the world. I consider you've both been very underhand about it, though."

"If you hadn't been so busy organizing my affairs for me, Katie, you might have observed that I had ideas of my own," said Simon mildly.

"Well, of course, Sarah's a dear, and she's like one of the family, and I'm very happy for you, but . . ."

"It's not what you expected," said Sarah, amused at the struggle Katie was having between her disappointment and her genuine wish for Simon's happiness. The pictures of the Italian villa were fast fading, and Sarah feared that she must seem a very unglamorous substitute for Anna.

Then Katie, with the quick change of mood so characteristic, gave Sarah a warm smile and said, "What a lukewarm reception we're giving to your news! You shouldn't spring such surprises on us, but Simon couldn't have chosen a nicer person to join the family. If only you'd given me a hint."

"My dear girl," said Simon, "we hardly ever see you. What did you expect Sarah to do? Keep sending you progress reports. We lack your liking for publicity where our personal feelings are concerned."

"Well, Max was the only one who had any inkling, and he wasn't sure."

Sarah's eyes sparkled as she looked at Max, and he gave her a wry smile as he said, "Don't mind following coffee with champagne myself. Never was a stickler for the rules. Count Katie and me in, Simon."

"Right," said Simon, and caught the wine waiter's eye.

After that, things went happily enough. If Max saw his financial help from Anna jeopardized, he was able to accept it philosophically and toasted them with a witty little speech. Katie, seeming to warm to the situation more and more as realization sunk in, sparkled gaily and forgave Simon his strictures.

Sarah did not see Anna again that evening, but as she was packing her case that night, Katie knocked at her bedroom door and came in, perching herself on the bed.

"Heavens, I'm exhausted! I've just been with Anna. She's in a frightful state. Pacing up and down her room like a tigress in a cage. You *have* upset her apple cart and no mistake. I've never seen her lose control like this. I guess she's not used to being on the losing side."

"She'd lost Simon before I came on the scene."

"She won't believe that."

"Do you?"

Katie plucked at the bedspread, troubled.

"You are sure, Sarah? About you and Simon, I mean. You see, it wasn't an ordinary casual sort of affair between him and Anna. It really went deep."

"Simon's told me about it. He has made it plain to Anna ever since she turned up again last Christmas that as far as he's concerned, it is dead. It can only be vanity that makes her refuse to believe it, or the desire of a spoiled child to have what is denied her. After all, if she cared so much for Simon, why did she marry another man? If his wealth and position and name meant more than Simon did, can she be surprised that Simon's feelings changed? She had her chance."

"That's no consolation, to know that you had it and passed it up. Only makes the desire to get it back again all the stronger. Second chances don't often come again, though," concluded Katie, as though she had reason to know.

"Anna would be wise to go back to her own country and forget Simon. She has so much to go back to. And can you imagine Simon being happy giving up his profession to live in Italy as a sort of retainer of Anna? He's not the kind of man to be contented with an idle, rich life."

"I bet he'd soon get used to it," said Katie wickedly. "I would."

"You'd be bored stiff after a short time."

"Perhaps. I'd like to give it a trial, though. Anyway, I do see that you're a sound choice for Simon, and I hope you'll both be very happy."

"A sound choice. That seems a little dull,

Katie," said Sarah, her eyes twinkling. "But I'll do my best."

"I never know when you're putting me on, Sarah. And if there's one word that doesn't apply either to you or Simon, it's dull. But whatever I say, I guess I put my foot in it. You need to stand up for yourself with Simon, though. Be warned."

"I knew that when I was seven."

"I suppose you'll live at Marlyn Manor so that you can look after father. He'll be a great burden. It's rather a shame. Lucky, though, that you get on so well with him."

"We haven't made any definite plans yet," said Sarah, folding a dress and putting it in her case.

"You're so nice, Sarah. Too nice for us Rannocks, perhaps. But it'll be good to have you in the family."

"I always had a soft spot for the Rannocks," said Sarah, as she snapped the locks of the suitcase.

Simon and Sarah breakfasted early the next morning, but the others came down in time to see them off, and Anna, in spite of Simon's vigilance, managed to corner Sarah on the porch while she was waiting for Simon to bring the car around. Anna looked a sickly color that morning and her eyes were puffy. Sarah guessed that she had not slept much that night. She spoke coolly, apparently well under control although a slight trembling in her voice betrayed the depth of her feeling. In her eyes, Sarah read a contemptuous hatred that chilled her.

"I wouldn't be too sure of your bargain. You don't imagine that Simon loves you, do you?"

"I keep my imagination for my writing," said Sarah lightly, but Anna was obviously not interested in anything Sarah might say, being intent only on getting her own view across before Simon returned.

"He's using you to look after his father and provide him with some sort of a home. Simon loves me. He always has, ever since the first day we met. If he goes through with this farce, you'll merely be his housekeeper and nurse for his father. He's got to have somebody for the old man. Mr. Rannock may go on for years yet, getting more helpless but refusing to leave that morgue of a house. If that's what you want ... I should have thought you could have made a better life for yourself than that. You're not without talent, I believe."

Stung by the patronizing tone of the last few words, Sarah said softly, "I have been told so. But it doesn't do to believe all that one is told."

"A marriage of convenience. You'll find that cold comfort."

"Did you?"

Anna stared at her angrily, but Sarah's steady eyes and calm expression seemed to curb her, for she hesitated, then said acidly, "A different matter altogether."

Simon drove up snappily and slid out of the car.

"Good morning, Anna. Give me that case, dear. It's too heavy for you."

He stowed the suitcase in the trunk of the car as Max and Katie came out into the porch to see them off. Simon, in no mood to linger, was driving out of the hotel entrance a few moments later.

"Sorry about that. Any claw marks?" he said.

"Not to worry. I'm glad the sun's shining for our drive home."

"Quite a momentous weekend."

"Yes."

"Happy? No qualms?"

"Happy," she said, and he laid his hand briefly on her knee as he accelerated down the lane.

But Sarah knew that she did bear a few intentional claw marks from Anna and one or two fainter, unintentional scratches from Katie.

CHAPTER FIFTEEN

THE COTTAGE GARDEN was full of color in the second week of May when Sarah finished her book. Wallflowers, tulips, and daffodils made the greatest contribution, with pockets of cowslips, polyanthuses and lilies of the valley scattered among them in true cottage garden confusion. The air was filled with the heavy scent of May blossom from the old tree at the end of the garden, and Jeff Murcia was muttering darkly about the low night temperatures and the damage that frost could do at that time of the year to young tender growth.

Walking around the garden with Piper in attendance, trying to relax after the fierce concentration she had brought to the conclusion of her book, she was conscious of feeling tired, and a little blank. She had been living with her characters for so long that it felt strange now to be finished with them. She could not judge at this stage how well she had brought it off. She would be able to tell better when she read it all through, but she was satisfied that it marked an improvement on her first book. Now she would be able to concentrate on the closing stages of Paul Rannock's memoirs. She had felt a little ragged lately, torn between his work, her own book, and her preoccupation with Simon.

Piper, who had been crouching in a patch of long grass, suddenly swarmed up the trunk of a laburnum tree as though fired by a rocket, balanced with apparent comfort on a narrow sloping branch, and dabbed with a gentle, tentative paw at a pendulant blossom. Smiling up at the little black cat in the shower of gold, Sarah felt her heart lift at the bounty of May. It would be good to have a little more leisure to enjoy the garden and the country at this, the loveliest time of the year.

Walking along the lane to Marlyn Manor the following afternoon, she heard the first cuckoo from a thicket across the river. Birds flitted busily in and out of the hedgerow, seeking food for their young. She would try to persuade Paul Rannock to walk round the garden with her after their working stint. He had seemed more tired than usual lately, his pallor more marked, and he seldom left the house these days. Perhaps the warm sunshine would tempt him.

But when she arrived, Mrs. Pilsen met her in the hall with the news that Mr. Rannock had locked himself in his study and did not want to be disturbed.

"Been there all day. Didn't want any lunch. Just a pot of tea."

"Is he ill?"

"No. Just wants to be left alone to work, he said. I'm sure I don't want to disturb him. It's the Women's Institute meeting today, so I'll be off now," said Mrs. Pilsen, with an injured air which suggested that whatever exchanges had passed between her and Paul Rannock had not been exactly affable.

Sarah knocked at the study door.

"It's me. Sarah," she said.

After a few seconds, she heard Paul Rannock's limping step and the door was unlocked.

"Hello, my dear. Bit off-color today. Shall have to leave you to it."

She was shocked by his appearance. Against the extreme pallor of his face, the long puckered scar stood out more markedly than ever, and his dark eyes burned from sunken sockets with an almost feverish light. She had grown used to his ravaged, disfigured face and saw only the kindness and friendliness there for her, and the loneliness, too. But that afternoon, it was different. He looked tormented, almost desperate.

"Can I get you anything?" she asked gently.

"No, thanks. I've left a few more pages on your desk. If you'll edit them. Take them home if you like. I shan't be fit for any more work today."

"I'll do it here. Call if you want me for anything," she said, and went through the study to the door which led into her small room. She looked back, her hand on the door handle, hesitating. He so obviously wanted to be alone and was so obviously ill. He slumped down at his desk, his back to her, and she left him, uneasily wondering what to do.

While she worked on his manuscript, the writing even more difficult than usual to read, she kept listening for any movement in the next room. She stopped when she thought she heard a whimper, like a dog. There was silence, and then it came again. She hesitated no longer and went into the study. At first she thought it was empty, then she saw him crouched in a corner, his arm shielding his eyes, his huge frame hunched and trembling, turned from the light. She went and knelt down beside him.

"No, no," he muttered, turning his face away into the angle of the wall.

"It's me. Sarah," she said gently, taking his hand.

He was trembling violently, but turned half fearfully at the sound of her voice. His eyes searched her face as though she were a stranger. His mouth moved but no words came.

"Sarah Rushden," she said.

"Martin," he mumbled.

"Martin's granddaughter. You're at home. You're quite safe," she said, putting an arm around his hunched shoulders.

She was playing it by instinct but somehow

seemed to have struck the right reassuring note, for he relaxed, dropped his arm, and slumped against her. She held him for a few moments; then he looked up and she saw recognition in his eyes.

"Sarah. Sorry. One of my turns. Thought I'd got over them. Forgive me."

"Stay there while I get your stick."

With the aid of his stick and her arm, he got to his feet and stumbled back to his desk. There he put his head in his hands.

"What can I get you?" asked Sarah, putting a hand on his shoulder.

"Brandy. And soda. In that cupboard."

The drink seemed to help him collect himself. Sarah watched him gravely, her heart aching for this man so racked with physical and mental pain.

"I'm so sorry to distress you, dear. I felt it coming on this morning and thought I could see it out alone. I forgot you were coming. Lost track of the days."

"I'm glad I was here, if it helped."

"You do help, always. No fuss. So gentle and kind. You mustn't worry about me, though. I get these nightmares now and again. Been free of them for a long time. Hoped I'd finished with them."

"You've got overtired. Working too hard on these memoirs lately."

"Perhaps. Only a small setback, though. Don't mention it to Simon. Don't want him worried. He's had enough."

"I think he ought to know."

"No. Please, Sarah. Don't rob me of my right of decision, too. I don't want Simon to be told. Just a small turn. Won't have the boy worried just as he's got an important job on hand in Spain. He's flying out on Monday, isn't he?"

"Yes."

"Promise, then. No mention of this."

"If that's your wish, I promise. After all, I shall be

here to pour your brandy," she added, smiling.

"Bless you, my dear. You can have no idea how happy your engagement to Simon has made me. The gods have relented, to grant me this favor at the end. Now I'm going up to bed. Feel exhausted. I didn't frighten you, did I?" he asked anxiously.

"How could you frighten me?" she said, and went to him and kissed him.

Deeply moved, he patted her shoulder and said with an odd smile, "Rannock and Rushden. It was always a good mixture."

And so, when Simon came to the cottage on Saturday, Sarah said nothing about his father's attack, although she felt a little bothered by her enforced silence. But work on plans for a small colony of villas in southern Spain had been absorbing him for some weeks past and she, too, did not want him to fly off to Spain with worries about his father dogging him.

"How long will you be away, Simon?" she asked, as they sat over tea in the garden.

"A couple of weeks probably. I'll leave you my hotel address and telephone number in case you need it. You've certainly brought some color into this garden since you've been here."

"Grandma Rushden would expect it of me."

He laughed.

"What a traditionalist you are! Where are we going to live when we're married, Sarah? Dad presents a problem. I have a flat. You have a cottage. Dad has Marlyn Manor. Quite a choice, but I hope we don't have to live in that bleak house of unhappy memory."

"We'll see when September comes."

"That engagement ring stays put as far as I'm concerned."

"Tell me again in September."

"I hope I'm not being weighed up and found

lacking in the desired qualities for a husband," he said, his eyes teasing her.

"I've known you a long time. Any weighing up was completed long since."

"All the same, I think I'll ask for some reassurance now," he said, moving along the garden seat to take her in his arms. She had been wanting that kiss for a long time, and they lingered over it. Then Simon released her and said, "Very nice reassurance, too. It's going to work out all right. You'll see."

Sarah wondered whether the reassurance would have taken so little time in the days of his love affair with Anna. In the weeks since their engagement, his attitude had changed little from the months that had preceded it. An affectionate friendship, a little teasing, a slightly more proprietary attitude, and always a practical manner. Perhaps she would not have minded the lack of any romantic element if Anna's words about a marriage of convenience had not stayed at the back of her mind, stabbing now and again like a thorny rose.

"By the way, I had a letter from Max yesterday," Simon went on. "He's decided that the cost of carrying out the plans I drew up for the cottage is too high and has called it off. I wasn't surprised. Wish he hadn't wasted my time, though."

But that episode had led to their engagement, she thought. Piper jumped on her lap and kneaded her thighs painfully before settling down with a purr. She stroked the top of his head with a gentle finger.

"You're quiet today," said Simon. "Anything wrong?"

"No. Just a bit used-up after finishing my book. It's like that. All zealous concentration while you're writing it, and then, when it's finished, wham, you feel like a doll with the sawdust running out, all limp and empty."

"M'm. I know the feeling. Get days like that

myself after a sticky job. Pleased with it? The book?"

"As pleased as one ever is with one's work. The day I feel completely satisfied with any book I write, I shall know I'm finished."

"Has it gone to the publishers?"

"No. I want to go through it, do a little revision perhaps. And find a title. Don't like the one I first thought of. I think I'll try out a few suggestions on Nick. He telephoned last night. He's coming down to see his cousin next weekend and said he'll look in on his way next Saturday to see how the book's shaped."

They were silent for a few minutes. Sarah hoped that Piper would not notice the fledgling blackbird she had seen hopping for shelter and concealment under a holly bush at the shrill command of its mother. All things about Piper enchanted her save his hunting instincts when it came to small birds. She was contemplating a collar with a small warning bell on it for him, but knowing Piper's fiercely independent nature, was not at all sure that he would accept it; and what Piper did not accept, he found ways of rejecting. She could not blame him for the instincts of his wild ancestors but winced nevertheless at the cruelty of nature just as she found so much joy and wonder in its beauty. In some dim way, she knew that the balance was necessary.

"Shall we go for a walk along the river before I go back to Bleak House? I want to have an hour or two with the old man before I leave tonight. He's looking a bit played out. He always does, of course, but seems a bit more so than usual, don't you think?"

"Yes. We've nearly reached the end of his memoirs. He'll be better when they're finished. I can do all the final revision and tidying up."

"Wish I could have stayed over the weekend, but I must get back to the flat tonight. I've some work to do tomorrow, as well as getting packed up. I'm leaving at six on Monday morning."

"Shall I come with you and see you off?"

"At that unearthly hour? Good grief, no! Heathrow is not exactly an appealing place, and you'd have a tiresome journey home."

He was right, of course, but she wanted to shorten the time of their separation as much as possible. Her feeling of oppression at the thought of his absence made her realize how deeply now he was knitted into her life. Having finished her book, her mind was free to miss him all the more.

The meadows on each side of the river were gold with buttercups. A heron, sitting on the river bank, moved away down river as they approached, his wide wings flapping slowly. White May blossom dotted the slopes and was thick in the little hollows that ran down to the river. The early evening sunshine burnished the water to pale gold as it flowed over its shallow bed of sand and pebbles.

"Peace," said Simon. "Pity me, sweating it out with builders and bulldozers and cement mixers on the site for the next two weeks."

"Some people would think southern Spain a good exchange."

"Building sites are building sites the world over, and I shan't have much time to spare for anything else. Besides, what can compare with England in May? I shall be glad to get back. See what a softening influence you have on me."

She smiled and squeezed his arm.

"I shall miss you."

When he left her that evening, he took her in his arms and kissed her.

"I'm thankful you're here to keep an eye on my father. Don't hesitate to telephone me if you're worried about anything. And look after yourself."

She wanted to cling to him, but he released her and got into his car. She stood at the gate, watching him drive down the lane and disappear around the bend. His parting words, she thought, might have been from an elder brother to a sister.

He had left her still with most of the evening to herself. To try to throw off the mood of disappointment and a depression most unusual for her, she changed into slacks and an old sweater and set about weeding the flower beds, which Jeff Murcia had been frowning at for some days past, for the surge of growth in May had been too swift for her to cope with in her limited free time.

CHAPTER SIXTEEN

THE FIRST OF the letters came two days after Simon's departure. The envelope was typewritten. Opening it over her breakfast coffee, Sarah's heart leaped at the first words, recognizing Simon's writing.

> *My dearest love,*
> *You will be back on your home ground now and I am left with the bleak prospect of a whole month without you, and only the recollection of the past two weeks together to warm me.*

As she read on, puzzled at first, her joy froze. It was a passionate love letter, too intimate for a third party to read, and yet before she had realized fully that she was not the one addressed, she had read it to the end. Then she looked at the date. It had been written on the first day of June five years ago. She picked up the envelope with a shaking hand and studied the postmark. The letter had been posted two days before in London. There was no covering note. Anna had simply put it in the envelope and addressed it to her.

All that day and that night, the words that Simon had written burned in her mind, as Anna had intended they should. In vain she told herself that it was an old affair, dead as far as Simon was concerned, and that she ought to put it out of her mind. But they were not the sort of words she could put out of her mind. She would not have thought him capable of exposing his feelings so nakedly. The man she knew kept his feelings on a tight rein.

The second letter arrived a week later. It came, as before, in a typewritten anonymous envelope with no comment. And try as she would not to read it, her eyes skimming over the pages took in his impassioned pleas to announce their engagement, to get married as soon as possible. "I want you for my own, as you want me. Why do you hesitate, my love?"

At first, her instinct had been to burn the letters. Then she had wondered whether to return them without comment to Anna, but she did not know her address nor did she wish to know it. The time must be close now for her return to her home in Italy. Was this a last desperate move to break their engagement or was it merely cruel malice toward Sarah herself? In the end she put the letters in the drawer of her grandmother's little bureau and tried in vain to forget them.

She received only one brief postcard from Simon during his absence, announcing his arrival and saying little else. The contrast was painful.

And then, two days before Simon was due to return, she arrived at Marlyn Manor to find Paul Rannock in bed.

"He's very poorly," said Mrs. Pilsen. "I suggested getting the doctor, but he'd have none of it."

When Sarah went up to his room, she found him in a weak state, barely conscious, and telephoned for the doctor.

"No good, dear," he whispered as she took his hand. "I'm on the way out. Not sorry, so don't grieve. Don't let them take me away. Want to die here, in my own home."

The doctor confirmed that there was little to be done. Paul Rannock's heart was failing. He suggested his removal to hospital.

"Not unless it will give him a chance to live," said Sarah.

"It can only prolong life for a few days. Perhaps not that. Quite frankly, I'm amazed that he's lasted as long as he has. I can arrange for a night nurse."

"I shall stay with him. How long do you think?"

The doctor shrugged his shoulders.

"A few hours. A few days. Difficult to be precise. Will you inform his family?"

"Yes."

He gave her a few brief instructions and left. When they were alone, Paul Rannock, who had appeared unconscious, opened his eyes and gave Sarah a faint, twisted smile.

"Never have gone much for the medics. Just as soon have a witch doctor. I finished a drawing for you. Downstairs in the study."

She stooped and kissed him.

"Don't tire yourself with talking. I'll go and get a hot drink for you; then I'll telephone Simon and Alison."

He nodded and closed his eyes. Later on, when he was sleeping and she had done all she could, she went into the study and found the drawing on his desk. A Cornish beach, huge granite boulders, curling waves, and receding into the distance four children running along the edge of the waves. The children were small, vague figures vanishing into the distance, having a dreamlike quality, as though he had been saying farewell. And she marveled again at his gift for evoking a mood, catching a moment on the wing, and holding it there on paper forever.

"The drawing," she said, late that evening when he was awake. "It's lovely. A dream."

He nodded and whispered,

"Given me so much pleasure—doing them. A

journey back into childhood. An unexpected bonus. Thank you, dear Sarah."

Those were the last words he spoke. Alison shared the night watch with her, but he slept peacefully. Simon arrived back the next morning. He took Sarah in his arms.

"You look all in. How is he?"

"Slipping peacefully away."

The three of them stayed by him until he died without regaining consciousness late that afternoon. Watching Simon's face as he stood at the foot of the bed looking at his father, she wondered what he was feeling about this man who had deserted his family and children for so many years and at so much cost to them and yet who had won, she thought, at the end, Simon's affection and respect.

Brian and Katie had been unable to get there.

"Brian's on holiday in Portugal and didn't propose to return until the end of the week. Katie's tied up with rehearsals. She'll ring up again tomorrow," Alison had said after she had contacted them.

Simon drove Sarah back to the cottage that evening. They were both silent on the way. She made a pot of tea and some toast, for they had eaten little that day.

"A release for him. He suffered a lot of pain from those injuries, you know. Never complained. Great courage," said Simon.

"Yes. We shouldn't be sad for him. But I shall miss him dreadfully."

Simon looked at her and nodded.

"Yes. You loved him. And he loved you. Not his own children, but you. Odd, that."

"He was fond of you. Anxious for your happiness. He had a great respect for you."

"We came to a good understanding in the end. Well, that's it, and we mustn't be morbid. You're looking tired out, my dear. I'm sorry I wasn't here when he was taken ill. I'd have liked to have been there when he was conscious."

"His mood was very peaceful, happy almost."

"Good. Now, apart from this sad business, how's my girl?"

"I'm all right. Did you finish what you went out to do?"

"Pretty well. I'll probably have to go again in the autumn."

He looked tired and talking seemed an effort. She had no intention of telling him about the letters. Quite apart from anything else, it would be painfully embarrassing for him to know that a third party had read what was meant only for Anna's eyes, words that he might even blush for himself now. Somehow, she must put them out of her mind. He would have much to see to in arranging for the funeral and clearing up his father's affairs. He would need her support, not a recurrence of the Anna affair in this painful and malicious form.

And then, the day after the funeral, the third letter came. This time a snapshot was enclosed with it. Simon, clad in light slacks and an open-necked shirt, was carrying a laughing Anna clad in a brief swimsuit. They were in what appeared to be a sandy cove. Anna's arms were round his neck and Simon was laughing down at her upturned face. A younger Simon, his face more rounded, the bones less prominent, his thick black hair rumpled in the wind. Who had taken it, she wondered? And had Anna sent her the original or had she ordered a second print for Sarah's benefit?

This time she managed to resist the temptation to read the letter, apart from a glimpse of some endearments and the date, and thrust it in the back of the drawer with the others, scarcely knowing why she could not bring herself to destroy them. They stayed there, leaking their poison into her. The date on this last letter indicated that he was writing at weekly intervals during Anna's four weeks in Italy. When the snapshot was taken, she had no idea. Perhaps on the two weeks' holiday together which had apparently preceded her departure for Italy. But why, she thought despairingly, must she analyze it all? Why let Anna's malice work by thinking about it, picturing it?

Now that Simon's father was dead, Anna might think her chances had revived. Katie would no doubt have told her. And Simon, she would think, would have no reason now for making that "marriage of convenience." And as the long, light days of June slipped away, Sarah began to wonder, too, whether Simon was thinking on similar lines, for she saw little of him, and when they did meet, he seemed preoccupied and distant.

Clearing up his father's papers, he found two letters in his desk, one for Sarah, one for himself. He brought them into the little room where she was working on the last chapter of Paul Rannock's memoirs. They had both been written two weeks before he died. Sarah's said:

My dear,
My time is running out, and I want to thank you for making the last months so much happier and more rewarding than I could ever have dreamed possible.

Your editorial work on my book has been invaluable, and I have arranged for you to have a fair reward, although no financial reward, even if I were a millionaire, could repay you for these past months of friendship. You could almost persuade me not to welcome the end. Almost.

And to know that you and Simon will be happy in your marriage, which I don't doubt—your grandparents' spirit and grace live on in you, and Simon will know how to appreciate that and benefit from it—is a great joy to me. You have my love,

P.R.

She handed the letter to Simon, her eyes bright with unshed tears. He read it, sitting on the corner of her desk, then gave it back to her.

"I saw the will at the lawyer's this morning. You are to have half of whatever the book earns. The rest is to be distributed among the family."

"I wanted no payment for what I've done, but it was kind and generous of him."

"He couldn't have written it without your help."

"You'll sell Marlyn Manor?"

"Yes. And all the contents. Is there any memento you'd like?"

She thought a moment, then said, "His drawings are the best memento I could have. And the book of poems he gave me. I shall remember him, always."

"Yes. An odd character. I admired his courage. We none of us really knew him, of course. Did you see this coming on, Sarah? Mrs. Pilsen hinted that he'd had one of his queer turns a few weeks back."

"I knew he was more than usually tired lately."

But he had noticed her initial hesitation and said sharply, "Nothing else?"

"He was in a distressed condition one afternoon, but it passed off."

"When was this?"

"Just before you went to Spain. He didn't want you worried."

"You should have told me."

"He didn't wish it."

"Maybe not, but you promised me."

"It doesn't matter now."

"I should have been told. It might have been the precursor to more attacks. You could have been at risk."

His tone was curt and she felt too vulnerable to take it just then so that her voice trembled a little as she said, "I had no difficulty in soothing him. Don't fuss now, Simon, please. I'm going to make a pot of tea."

He tightened his lips but said no more about it. Over tea, he passed her the letter his father had left him.

Dear Simon,

The natives always knew when death was round the corner, and I must have picked it up from them. So just a few words of thanks for your patience and care. Much in the past to ask forgiveness for, and much that you couldn't possibly understand, but you have been generous and without reproach. But 'The devil was sick, the devil a monk would be,' etc. I can't play the penitent now that I'm helpless and sick when I know that, given my life over again, I would no doubt do just the same. My sin was in not knowing myself well enough when I was young. I was never made for the domestic yoke. Not that I can't see the rewards, given the right partner.

You will have that. My blessings on you both. My biggest, perhaps my only regret, is that my wanderings made my eldest child a stranger to me from childhood, and put burdens on him which were properly mine. His kindness and help for this ailing egotist are all the more praiseworthy.

Cherish Sarah. She will bring you happiness, which I fancy is overdue.

Yours, in gratitude,
P.R.

Sarah handed it back to him silently. A chapter had closed, she thought. And Paul Rannock had made his exit with calm courage and generosity of spirit.

CHAPTER SEVENTEEN

WITH SIMON OCCUPIED clearing things out at Marlyn Manor and putting the house on the market while he coped with an unusually busy spell in his office, it was not surprising that he had little time for her, but unfortunately it had all come at a time when she needed reassurance from him more than ever before.

The fourth letter arrived from Anna on the last day of June. Sarah had come down that morning with a headache and a feeling of oppression, which the close, gray morning did nothing to lift. The air felt thundery after two or three days of hot weather, and even Piper seemed lethargic, greeting her with less than his usual show of affection, and instead of bounding out of the back door when she opened it, merely walking down the step and straightway sitting down, his tail curled neatly round his paws, surveying the world with a disillusioned stare.

That Saturday loomed blankly before her as she buttered her breakfast toast. Simon had been away in the Midlands for the previous few days and did not expect to be back in time to see her that weekend. Some unfavorite chores awaited her, put off while she was busy with her book and Paul Rannock's memoirs, but now looming large with no excuse for further postponement. She also was plagued with an inability to come up with a title for her book which pleased both publisher and herself, her latest having been rejected, with the utmost kindness, by Mr. Birch owing to the regrettable fact that the same title had already been used for a book still in print. But over and above all, she was unhappy at Simon's seeming neglect although she knew there were good rational reasons for it. She was simply not in a rational mood, she decided, and then saw the postman come up the path with a letter in his hand.

She knew as soon as she saw it on the mat and was annoyed with herself for feeling sick and shaken at the sight of it. In a mood of defiance at such a craven spirit, she resisted the first impulse to put it unopened with the rest and masochistically read it. If only, she thought, those words were addressed to her. When she had finished reading it, she felt as though her heart had been put through a mincing machine.

In a morbidly self-denigrating mood, she blamed herself for everything. It was she who had put Simon in this impossible position by suggesting the engagement. Embarrassed by it, unwilling to hurt her, he did not know how to bring it to an end, now that circumstances had changed and he had had time to regret his chivalrous offer to make it no sham but a binding reality. She must put it right. At least give him the chance to get out of his predicament without embarrassment. She had merely helped him get out of one predicament into another, but at least she would not dog him like Anna.

And so, a little later that morning, having rehearsed in her mind what she would say, she sat down at her desk in the small room at the back of the cottage, which was her writing room, and tried to compose a letter which would make it easy for him. It must at all costs avoid being emotional. He had experienced more than enough emotional scenes in his time. She would like to say, "I love you. I want nothing so much as to be loved by you. But this is not to be, and I would sooner have a good friendship with you than an unhappy marriage." But that would make him feel guilty. So she masked her feelings and wrote instead,

> Dear Simon,
> I feel that now circumstances have changed with the death of your father, you may wish to be free of our bargain before the agreed closing date. I wouldn't want you to feel bound in any way. You, who have been bound by obligations for most of your life. I hope I have helped to free you of one entanglement, which was the original idea. I feel I was wrong to offer that solution, though. It has put you in an awkward position, and you are too kind, and fond of me, too, I believe, to want to hurt me.
> I'm afraid that if matters drift on, our friendship may be affected. Lately, I've felt a distance between us. Rather than have that happen, I would prefer to put the clock back to before that Cornish holiday. No need to feel guilty in any way. It was all my doing.
> I am writing because I seem to see so little of you these days. So back to square one, and please come to Rylands as often as you can. I cherish our friendship.
>
> Yours,
> Sarah

Although large drops of rain were starting to fall from a sullen sky, she ran down the lane to the post box before she could change her mind, and spent the rest of the day in an anguished state, realizing that Anna had achieved what she had set out to do.

All that weekend, she felt doomed. Doggedly forcing herself to perform the neglected chores, she turned out cupboards, relined kitchen drawers with new paper, washed kitchen and bathroom curtains, and generally made a martyr of herself.

On Monday, half expecting a telephone call from Simon all day, she busied herself in the garden, where the violent storms of the weekend had brought down rambler roses and created havoc in the borders. It would happen, she thought, just when the flowers in the border were at their best and the roses laden with bloom. As she looked at the delphinium spikes broken and beaten to the ground and the trailing thorny branches of battered roses, she felt it typified life. Just when hopes were highest, dreams idyllic, came the storm to ruin all.

Twice she ran into the cottage, thinking she heard the telephone, only to meet with silence. Why should he telephone, anyway, she asked herself. He was busy. Would write in his own time.

She was turning out the bureau that evening, lingering, in spite of herself, over the letters which had so poisoned her days, trying to bring herself to destroy them, when the heavy door-knocker shattered the silence and made her jump. It would be Simon, she thought, and hastily rammed the letters under the blotter on the desk before going to the door.

He came into the hall as though nothing had happened, and said, "Hello. Sorry I couldn't get round this weekend. Didn't drive back until yesterday evening. Have you been crying?" he asked, as he went into the sitting room and faced her in the evening light of that sunny room.

"No."

"Your eyes are puffy."

"Had a bonfire this afternoon. There was a good deal of damage from the storm. I burned a lot of green stuff."

He sat down in the armchair opposite her and

eyed her with an expression that she didn't much like. A cool, raking look.

"You're quite well, then?"

"Of course I am," she said impatiently. "Why do you ask?"

"Thought you might be suffering from overstrain when I read that odd, ambiguous letter of yours."

"I thought it was plain enough."

"Well, I'm sorry if I'm stupid. Perhaps you'll spell it out for me in simpler words. What exactly has my father's death to do with our engagement?"

This, she thought, was going to be very difficult. She knew these cool moods of Simon that made one feel like a small mouse under a harrow.

"Well," she began, and stopped.

"Go on. I'm not going to say it for you."

Too late, she realized what a hole she had dug for herself. Why hadn't she taken more care with the phrasing of that letter? She looked at him appealingly.

"Go on, Sarah," he said softly. "A simple answer to a simple question. What has my father's death to do with our engagement?"

"I thought that now you were free of that responsibility . . ." Again she stopped, then stumbled on. "I thought your reasons for wanting to marry would be weakened."

"Not like you to be so mealy-mouthed. Are you trying to tell me that I wanted you not so much for a wife as a nurse and keeper for my father?"

She was silent, and he went on. "I see. Is that an original thought or was it put into your head by someone else? I find it hard to stomach that you believe I was using you in that fashion, for cheap, unpaid help."

"I'm sorry, Simon. I've made an awful mess of it. And I was only thinking of you."

"What an odd way of thinking of me. Will you try to explain a bit further?"

His acid politeness hurt more than any overt anger.

"I thought you were regretting our bargain. That you were too chivalrous, to use an old-fashioned word but I can't think of another, to tell me. That I'd only got you out of one entanglement to put you in another. About my usefulness in looking after your father. No, that wasn't an original thought. It was put to me first by Katie. She told me that was Anna's reading of the situation. And Anna herself repeated it to me just before we left the hotel in Cornwall."

"And you believed it?"

"No, not really. Only don't you see, Simon?" she said desperately. *"I* made the engagement offer to you. The wrong way round. Because of that, I needed more reassurance. I feel that you're fond of me, but I know that you don't love me. Not as you loved Anna. And I think people need to love each other to make a success of marriage. You know and I know, from our parents' experience, what a sad business it can be otherwise. And lately, there's been a distance between us. I thought you were realizing that friendship wasn't enough."

"If you say that there's been a distance between us lately, and I don't deny it, that cool little letter of yours was an odd way of trying to lessen it."

And at that moment the telephone rang in the hall. It was Nick, who had been doing some research for her on some references in the last pages of Paul Rannock's memoirs which she had not understood. She fetched a sheet of paper from the bureau, with a hurried explanation to Simon, and returned to the telephone to take some notes.

In her absence, Simon lit a cigarette and leaned back in the chair, his face thoughtful. Piper had jumped up on the bureau and was engaged in delicately pawing a shiny piece of paper protruding from under the blotter. Simon, idly admiring the little cat's patience and dexterity, watched him paw out the object of his attention and pat it on to the floor, where he tapped it along playfully for a few moments, then lost interest and set about washing his rear leg with sudden fervor. Simon went to pick up what he now saw was a snapshot in order to return it to the bureau, and stared at it, frowning. When he heard Sarah coming back, he put it in his pocket.

"Sorry about that," she said. "Where were we?"

"Still trying to sort out why you wrote that odd letter. You know, Sarah, one of the things I love you for is your honesty. Previously, we've always met on a frank, honest footing. If I've annoyed you, you've told me why. All open and above board. Recently, it's been different. You've been holding back. I put it down to grief over my father. I know he meant a lot to you. I thought you were brooding over it. And I've been unavoidably occupied with my father's affairs as well as a sudden rush of work so haven't been able to be with you as much and find out what's behind it. It seemed to start while I was away. When I found that you'd hidden the true state of my father's health from me in spite of the promise you made, I felt vaguely that our old frankness with each other, confidence in each other if you like, had evaporated."

"We didn't want to worry you, Simon, just as you were going away. Your father asked me not to deny him the right of making his own decisions. I couldn't refuse him."

"You should have, because his health denied him that right. It could have been disastrous. Perhaps I should have made it clearer at the start, but I thought I'd said enough to let you know the true state of affairs. Do you realize he might have injured, even killed you, when he was not responsible for his actions?"

"No, that would never have happened. I had no difficulty in getting him to recognize me."

"I took a chance that those fits would not recur, but I was given some pills to use if there were any symptoms of a return. No use giving them to my father to keep by him. He would have thrown them out. That was why I asked you to let me know. I'd have left the pills with you. Warned the doctor. No use tracking back. It didn't happen, thank God. But it could have. And it shook me that you kept it from me. What else has been going on underneath the surface, Sarah? If we're to sort this out, you must tell me. Piper just dislodged this from your bureau."

"Oh, no!"

"Anna must have sent it to you. True?"

"Yes."

"What else?"

"Letters, from you to her."

"Show them to me."

Silently, she fetched the letters and handed them to him.

"Good grief!" he said disgustedly. "The . . ." He checked himself and glanced through them. "When did they come?"

"One a week, starting just after you left for Spain."

"You read them?"

"Yes. I tried not to, but I started the first one before I realized it wasn't addressed to me. And then I couldn't stop. I'm sorry."

"Why didn't you tell me before?"

"I thought it would be too painful for you. Too embarrassing."

"I'm not such a tender plant as you, dear. Embarrassing? Yes, to be reminded what a fool I was and to have it revealed to the one person whose opinion I value more than anybody's. But healthy, no doubt. Like seeing oneself going all tragic and dramatic about being mortally ill when it turns out to be merely an attack of mumps. Come, Sarah, where's that rational good sense of yours? You wanted to spare my feelings, and yet you hurt them far more by that letter than by revealing these romantic remnants of old folly."

"I haven't felt very sensible lately," she admitted forlornly.

He shook his head.

"And you, my anchor sheet. Do you know what this cottage, and you, have come to stand for in my life? A refuge of warmth and kindness and honesty and sane values in a crazy world. I thought of it constantly while I was away. Felt it like a nugget of gold hidden in my pocket. Thought that at last, at last, I was lucky enough to have a chance of real happiness. Nothing like the mad fever that gripped me during those years with Anna. Something good and durable."

"If only you'd written that instead of a brief card! I had nothing to fight those letters with."

"Yes, I forgot that as well as being a fountain of good sense, you are also a woman. I'm not good now at putting my feelings into words. I think perhaps Anna did that to me. Dried me up. Made me mistrust words. I felt that somehow you would understand without words. Remiss of me. But foolish of you to hide things from me, even if you did it to spare my feelings.

Her eyes danced. Suddenly, it was as though an enormous black cloud that had been obscuring her vision had lifted, and she felt that she could see clearly again after a period of hallucinations.

"It was marvelous stuff. Swinburne would look

pallid beside it. You've never thought of writing romantic fiction? It would go down well."

He took her in his arms and ruffled her hair.

"Although I confess to feeling ashamed, any ungenerous needling from you on the subject will be suitably punished. It's good to see the laughter back in your eyes, though. Another thing I love you for. Your sense of humor. Quite a lot of things, now I come to think of it."

"Dear Simon. I love you, too."

"Then, since we are quite clear about the only thing that matters, shall we get married soon?"

"Yes, please."

"And live here in this cottage? Plenty of space to build on to it if we want to. You seem to belong here, and there's something special about Rylands. It has a tradition of love and happiness. While I was away, I kept thinking of those lines of Davies. You know, 'My walls outside must have some flowers.' And saw you here."

"Yes, I love Rylands. Part of our past—the happiest part. I'd like it to hold our future, too. Carry on the tradition."

"And I suggest we tear up these highly colored reminders of my past foolishness and put the pieces on your next bonfire. And never believe, my love, that that affair was ever comparable with what we feel for each other. It was a mad obsession of the senses, a lust to possess. It would never have lasted six months if Anna had married me. Hopelessly incompatible."

"Has she returned to Italy?"

"Goes next week. I had a letter from her asking me to let bygones be bygones. Promising no more scenes. Would I have dinner with her before she leaves and perhaps come and pay her a visit at the end of the summer. She would love to show me her home. All sweetness and light."

"Have you replied?"

"Not yet. I suppose she thought her letters might have softened you up. Caused a rift. I'll send a brief note to let her know that we shall be too busy getting married to accept any social commitments this summer."

He put the torn pieces of the letters in the waste basket and, turning back to her, took her in his arms and kissed her, with a tenderness in his face that she had never seen before. Then he passed a finger gently under her eyes.

"Was it really the bonfire?"

"No."

"I'm sorry. I find it hard now to put my deepest feelings into words. I should have tried. Then you'd have had something to shore yourself up with against Anna's tunneling. Forgive me, I'll try to do better in future. And although I mistrust my own words to express my feelings, I'm not above borrowing other people's. I heard a poem read over the radio a few weeks back, and two lines have stayed with me because they say just what I feel for you.

*'I love thee to the level of every day's
Most quiet need, by sun and candlelight.'*

Will that do?"

"That will do beautifully, my love," said Sarah, and kissed him again.

He held her quietly for a few moments, both of them deeply moved, both savoring the peace of those moments after the emotional stresses of the past weeks. Piper, bored with this state of affairs, broke the spell by swarming up Sarah's back and perching precariously in the neighborhood of one shoulder while he piped his protest.

"That cat," observed Simon, "has no tact. We'd better acquire a dog to occupy his attentions. Come and show me what you've been doing in the garden before I make an ass of myself by trying to express the extremely mushy state of my mind just now."

And arm-in-arm, with Piper at their heels, they went out into the cool evening air of the garden.

BONUS BOOK OFFER

Send three coupons from the back of Pinnacle's Aston Hall Romance books, together with your cash register receipt(s) indicating proof of purchase, and we will send you the very next Aston Hall Romance ABSOLUTELY FREE! Please allow 6 weeks for delivery. Offer void June 30, 1981.

PINNACLE BOOKS, INC.—Bonus Book Offer
2029 Century Park East, Suite 1000, Los Angeles, CA 90067

Name _____

Address _____

City _____ State/Zip _____